Kung Fu Apprentice

Ryan Cansdale

This book is dedicated to all those who love Martial arts

Contents

Chapter 1 Feeling lost 1

Chapter 2 The Journey Starts 21

Chapter 3 Serious Training 48

Chapter 4 This Time It's Personal 68

Chapter 5 Re-opening *The Dark Panther* 93

Chapter 6 Strange Things Are Happening 113

Chapter 7 This Has Got To Stop 130

Chapter 8 The Mafia Boss 155

Chapter 9 Deception 180

Chapter 10 Escaped 204

Chapter 11 The Legend Continues 230

Chapter 1
Feeling lost

"Don't run down the stairs Ryan" Sally, my mom said as I ran into the kitchen and sat down at the end of the table. Noise filled the kitchen from my six brothers and six sisters. My mom came over to the table and placed a huge bowl of spaghetti sauce in the center. She went back to the counter and got another huge bowl that had spaghetti noodles in it.

She placed the noodles beside the sauce and sat down at the other end of the table. "Eat up before it gets cold" she said as she patiently waited until everyone grabbed some. Once everyone grabbed some, she heaped a few scoops onto her plate.

"So, how was everyone's day?" she asked as she took a bite. "Strong and I got on the basketball team" Cliff said as he gave Strong a high five. "That's great, looks like all that hard work paid off" my mom said as she smiled. "Jenny, Shay and I made the cheerleading team" Cutey said. "Wow, that's fantastic" Sally said as she clapped her hands.

"The teacher chose Dream, Jay, Dish and I to be in the upcoming play. It's about a teenage boy who has amnesia and searches for his home" Mike explained. "Wow, that sounds interesting, let me know when that is and I'll definitely come see it" she said with excitement in her voice.

"Rose and I got to play a piano solo in class today" Kate said. "I am sure it sounded beautiful" she said as she reached out and touched Kate's hand. "What about you hunny? Anything interesting happened to you?" she asked as she looked at me.

"No, just the usual homework" I said as I hung my head. "Don't worry Ryan, eventually something interesting will happen to you" Mike said. "Shut up Mike" I said as I clenched my fist. "Now now, you two play nice" my mom said as she raised her voice.

I was still eating when everyone got up and ran out of the kitchen. Cliff and Strong went to practice their basketball shots. Mike,

Dream, Jay and Dish went to rehearse their lines. Jenny, Shay and Cutey went to practice their cheerleading routine. And Rose and Kate went to practice on the piano. "Looks like you're stuck helping me with the dishes" Sally said as she got up.

I collected the plates from the table, rinsed them off and put them in the dishwasher. I filled the sink with soapy water and started to wash the pots. Sally grabbed a towel and helped. "Ryan, if your dad was still alive, he would tell you to find something that you're passionate about, something that really interests you" she said.

"I don't know what that is, nothing interests me" I said as I looked sad. "There must be something that you want to do, something that you're passionate about" she said. "Well, I have always found science interesting, maybe I could be a scientist" I said with hope in my eyes. "Okay, well at least that's something, so maybe you want to pursue that" she said as she took a dish from me and dried it.

I went upstairs, opened up my notebook and started my homework. The sound of the piano drove me to get up and walk down the hall. I banged on Kate and Rose's door. Kate opened the door. "What is it?" she asked. "I can't concentrate with all that noise" I said. "Well too bad, we have to practice" she said.

"I need to get this stuff done by tomorrow" I continued. "Too bad" she said as she closed the door. I went back to my room and tried to concentrate, but I couldn't. I picked up my notebook and books and walked downstairs. Jenny, Shay and Cutey were practicing their cheerleading routine.

"What are you doing here?" Shay asked. "I need to get this homework done" I said. "Well, we're practicing here" Cutey said. "I see that, but I really need to get this done" I said adamantly. "Come back in two or three hours, we'll be done then" Jenny said. "Fine" I said as I walked back upstairs.

I decided to go to the local coffee bar, which would be quiet I thought. I walked five blocks to *The Black Cup.* I ordered myself a coffee, found a quiet spot at the back corner next to the window and opened up my books. I began doing my homework. Ah, this is better, no noise, delicious cup of coffee, life couldn't get any better, I thought.

I was in the middle of writing, when a waitress came up to me. "Can I get you anything else sir?" she asked. I looked up and saw a tall, slender, black haired woman, who looked like she was in her early twenties. "No thank you" I said. "Okay, if you need anything else, just give me a holler" she said as she turned around and walked away.

I closed my books, got up and walked out the door. It was cold so I walked home at a fast pace. I went up the stairs to my room. I flopped on my bed and opened a book that I was in the middle of. I heard a knock at my door and I opened it. "Okay, the basement is free for you now" Cutey said.

"It's okay, I got my homework done" I said. "Did you find a nice quiet spot?" she asked. "Yes, I went to *The Black Cup*, that coffee shop a few blocks down the street" I said. "That's good" she replied. I shut the door and picked up my books. I could still hear the sound of the piano, but it didn't bother me.

I heard another knock on my door and I went to open it. "Hey Ryan, do you want to shoot some hoops with Strong and me?" Cliff asked. "Ya, let's go" I said as I followed them down the stairs and out the back door. "We are playing horse, whatever I do, Strong and you have to copy it exactly" Cliff said as he chucked me the ball.

"You go first and we have to copy you" he continued. I chucked the ball from the side of the house and missed the net completely. "Wow, where was that one going?" Strong asked. "Let me show you how a pro does it" he taunted. He shot the ball from where I was standing. It soared through the air and dropped in the net without touching the sides.

"Let see you do that" he said as he threw me the ball. I jumped and threw the ball at the net, it hit the side of the net and bounced off. "Looks like you're an H" he said with a smile on his face. He chucked the ball to Cliff. "Okay Cliffy, let's see what ya got" he said. Cliff threw it from the same spot and it went in effortlessly. He chucked the ball to Strong.

"Give me a harder one next time" he said. Strong ran up to the net and did a layup. It went in and he chucked the ball to me. I ran up for the layup, but I shot the ball too hard and it went right over the net. "Alright, that's an O for you Ryan" he said. I scooped the ball up and threw it to Cliff. He ran up to the net, but stumbled on the way and dropped the ball. "You're an H, Cliff" Strong laughed. "I'll get you, just you wait" Cliff threatened. "Watch this" Strong said as he lifted his left leg and threw the ball underneath and sunk the ball in the net.

I threw the ball underneath my left leg, the ball flew through the air and completely missed the net. "You're an R, Ryan" Strong teased. "Don't worry Ryan, we'll get him" Cliff said as he shot the ball under his left leg and it went in. "I can't believe it" Strong said. "Well, believe it, because it just happened, you're an H" Cliff said as we high fived.

"Alright, I guess I'm going to have to step it up a notch" he said. He sat down on the grass and chucked it in the net. I sat down on the grass as he threw the ball to me. I threw the ball and it didn't even make it to the net. "You know what that is Ryan, don't you?" Strong asked. "That is an S" he said.

Cliff sat in the same spot and chucked the ball. It hit the rim of the net and bounced off. "Damn" he shouted. "That an O for you" Strong said. Strong stood backwards and threw it from the far right as it dropped in the net with ease. I threw it backwards from the same spot, but it hit the backboard and bounced off. "Looks like you're a HORSE" Strong said as he laughed. "We'll get him next time" Cliff said as he looked at me. I walked in the house as the two of them continued to shoot hoops.

"Cookies are ready" Sally yelled as everyone ran into the kitchen and sat at the table. Sally set two trays in the center and we all took two. "Thanks mom" we all said at once. "I'll be home late tomorrow, I have a doctor's appointment" she said. "What about?" Cutey asked. "It's kind of personal" she said. "There is pizza in the freezer downstairs. Put it in the oven at five o'clock, I should be home around six thirty" she said.

"Alright, everyone get ready for bed" she said. We all got up and went to our rooms. "Goodnight" we all said as we turned our heads. Sally waited half an hour and went to say goodnight to us all. She walked up to Kate and Rose's room. She knocked on the door and went in.

Both the girls were in their beds. "You guys are sounding pretty good on that piano" she said. "Thanks mom" they both said. "Goodnight, love you" she said as she turned off their light and walked out of the room. "Love you" they both said. She walked to my room, walked inside and found me in my bed reading. "Time for bed sweetie" she said. "Okay" I said as I put the book on my nightstand. "Goodnight, love you" she said as she turned off the light and walked out.

She walked down the stairs and headed for Cliff and Strong's room. She walked in and found them talking about basketball. "Alright guys, time for bed, you have school tomorrow" she said as she turned off their light. "Good night mom, love you" Strong said. "Love you too hun" Sally said.

She walked down the stairs to the basement and found Mike, Dream, Jay and Dish still rehearsing for their play. "Okay boys, that's enough for one day, time to rest those eyes" she said. "Okay mom" Dish said as they ran to their room and hopped in their beds.

Sally walked down the hallway and into Kate, Shay and Cutey's room. She found them already sleeping and closed the door. She walked past the boys' room. "Goodnight guys, love you" she said as she walked upstairs. She turned off all the lights and went to her room. She brushed her teeth and climbed into her bed. She kissed a picture of her husband and closed her eyes.

She awoke to the sound of her alarm clock. It was seven, she sprang out of bed and ran into our rooms. "We overslept, you are going to be late for school, hurry up" she said. We all jumped out of bed, threw on our clothes and dashed downstairs to the table.

"I hope we're not late" Dream said. Sally threw on some eggs and toast. She quickly put it on the table. "Hurry and eat up" she said as she ran upstairs to get herself ready. "Bye mom" we all yelled as we started to put on our shoes. She ran downstairs and gave us all a kiss on the cheek.

"Bye, love you" she said as she ran back upstairs. We all walked out the front door. Jenny, Shay, Cutey, Mike, Dream, Jay, Dish and I started to walk the seven blocks to our school. Cliff, Strong, Elizabeth, Kate and Rose went and sat at the bus stop.

On the walk to school, everyone was talking about what they were all doing together. I didn't talk to anyone, because I wasn't involved in their activities. I was quiet all the way to school. We all walked in the front door and went off in different directions. We didn't even say goodbye to each other.

I walked down the hall towards my locker. I unlocked it, got my books out and started to head to my first class. On the way, I saw the school bully coming straight for me. "Where are you going nerd?" he asked as he smacked my books on the ground. As I bent down to pick them up, he kicked me and I fell to the ground. "See you later nerd" he said as he walked away.

Some people looked at me, but just walked on by like nothing happened. I tried to straighten out my papers, but they were all messed up. I walked into class, sat down at my desk and tried to sort them out. "Keep your papers organized" the teacher said as he walked past my desk. I started to say that it wasn't my fault, but he walked away.

The teacher handed out a test as everyone moaned and groaned. "That's enough" the teacher said. "This test will count for five percent of your overall mark, so take it seriously" he said as he sat down at his desk. I looked at the test and began to fill in the answers. The answers were just flowing out of me, my homework was paying off.

"Okay, pencils down, hand them to the front of the class" the teacher said twenty minutes later. I felt confident that I knew the material. I heard grumbling coming from behind me. "That was brutal" John said as he passed his test up to the front. "How did you find it?" he asked. "I think I did well" I said. "You sound overly confident" he said.

"I am, because I know the material" I said back. He didn't know how to respond to my comment so he stopped talking. Just then the bell rang, everyone got up and walked out the door. "I will have these marked for you by tomorrow" the teacher said as we were passing his desk. "I am not looking forward to that" John said as he looked at me.

I walked into math class, sat down and took out my books. "Listen up everyone, today we are getting a new student, she is transferring from Widdletown High" the teacher said. As soon as she walked in I recognized her. She was the waitress from the coffee shop. "Everybody welcome Kara to the class" the teacher said.

"Welcome Kara" we all shouted. "Find a seat" the teacher said as she handed Kara a text book. She glanced at the class and saw me and she sat down in the empty seat beside me. She turned to me and smiled. "Hey, remember me?" she asked. "Ya I do, you work as a waitress at *The Black Cup*" I said. "I didn't think that you were still in school. You look like you are in your early twenties" I said. "No, I am seventeen" she said. "How about you?" she asked. "I'm sixteen" I replied.

The bell rang for lunch as Kara turned to me. "I hope to see you at *The Black Cup* sometime" she said. "You will, I go there quite often" I said. "See you later" she said. I walked to the lunch room and saw Jenny, Shay, Cutey and Mike at a table. I went over and joined them. "Hi guys" I said. "Hi Ryan" they said.

"Where is the rest of the group?" I asked. "They are in class working on some homework" Cutey said. "How is your morning, good?" Shay asked. "Good, except that stupid bully knocked my books out of my hands and the teacher yelled at me for not having my papers organized" I said. "That guy is such a jerk, I've seen him pick on kids" Mike said. "Do you want me to kick his ass?" Cutey asked jokingly. "Ya, if you can" I teased back.

The rest of the day went by really fast. The bell rang and I found my brothers and sisters waiting out front for me. We walked home, talking about our day and laughing at jokes that we told. "We should practice our play some more tonight" Mike said to Dream, Jay and Dish. They all nodded in agreement.

"We have the house to ourselves until mom gets home" Cutey said. "Sweet, pizza night" I yelled. We walked in the front door and found that the others got home first. Jay immediately went downstairs and came up a moment later carrying five frozen pizzas. "I'll let these sit for a bit and I'll turn on the oven" he said. "Come on" he said as he waved Mike, Dream and Dish downstairs. Cliff and Strong went out back to practice basketball.

Elizabeth, Kate and Rose went to their room to practice the piano. Jenny, Shay and Cutey went to the living room to practice their cheerleading routine. I went up to my room and started to read my book. The oven started to beep, I ran downstairs and threw the pizzas in. I went back to reading and before I knew it, the pizzas were done. I shouted to everybody and a moment later they all came running.

We all grabbed a few slices and sat down at the table. "Let us perform our play for you guys" Mike said. "Okay, we can be your critics" Elizabeth said. "Hey, you got more than me" "Dish said as he looked at Strong's plate. "If you want it, you have to be faster than that" Strong replied. We all heard the front door open. "Mom" Cutey said as her, Jenny and Shay ran to meet her.

"Hi darlings" she said. "Can you help me with these groceries?" she asked. They picked up some bags and carried them to the kitchen counter. Strong, Mike and I helped with carrying the rest. Sally sat down at the table with us all. "Awesome, you saved me some" she said. "Of course, we wouldn't forget about you" Elizabeth said. "Is everything okay?" Kate asked.

"Everything's fine sweetheart. "That's good" Kate replied. "I had such a busy day today, you guys have no idea" she said. "Patient after patient, I didn't even get a break. I need to relax in a hot bath after" she continued. "How was everyone's day?" she asked. "Good" we all replied. "That bully really pissed me off, he walked up to me and knocked my books on the floor. And to top it all off, my teacher yelled at me for not having my books organized" I said.

"That sucks, just avoid him if you can" Sally said. "We all are going to watch Mike, Dream, Jay and Dish's play, you should come watch before your bath" Rose said. "Okay, sounds like fun" Sally said. We all finished, got up, put our plates in the dishwasher and went downstairs. We watched them perform their play. When it was done, we all clapped. "That was awesome" Jenny said. "Ya, I thought it was really well thought up and performed" Strong said.

I took off to *The Black Cup,* with my homework in my hand. I ordered myself a coffee and sat down. I opened up my notebook and began to work. After a while Kara came over. "Hey Ryan, do you want any more coffee?" she asked. "No thanks, I'm good" I said. "Sorry I can't talk, we are really busy" she said.

"Ya, I see that" I said. "I'll see you tomorrow, let's sit together at lunch" she said. "Okay" I said. "Have a good night" she said as she walked back to the coffee bar. I sat there for another three hours, until finally I was done my homework. There was still a line up as I walked out the door and headed home.

The next morning, the bus came at the usual time to pick up Cliff, Strong, Elizabeth, Kate and Rose. "Here, I saved you a seat Lizzy" one of the boys said who had a crush on her. "No thanks, I'll find my own seat" she said as she walked on by. She sat in the back with Rose. "He likes you" Rose said. "Ya, I don't like him" Elizabeth said. The bus arrived at the school and they all got off.

They sat on the grass in front of the school until the bell rang. When the bell rang, they all went to their first class that they all had together. They were the first ones there, so they all sat together. As the students started to pour in, the teacher entered. "Okay, everyone take your seats, who can tell me the answer to yesterday's problem?" he asked.

"In case you forgot, the problem was, what happens when you mix baking soda with vinegar?" he continued. "Yes" he said as he pointed to a girl with her hand up. "It causes a reaction with each other and it violently erupts" she said. "Correct" the teacher said. "Today we are going to experiment with these products" he continued.

At the end of the day, they waited for the bus at the bus stop. They stepped off the bus and walked in the front door. "That's odd, Ryan and the others usually beat us home" Kate said. "I'm not too worried about it" Cliff said as he sprawled out on the living room couch. "Move over" Rose said as she nudged her way on. Cliff turned on the television and the rest of them sat on the other couch.

Half an hour later, we walked in the door. "Hey, where were you guys?" Elizabeth asked. "We had to wait for Jenny and Shay because they got detention" Cutey said. "Where's mom?" Shay asked. "Good question" Strong replied. We searched the house for her. I went into the kitchen and found a note.

I have to work a double shift tonight, there is lasagna in the fridge and ice cream in the freezer, see you tomorrow, love mom. "I found a note" I yelled as they all rushed to read it. "Well, looks like we have the place to ourselves for the night" Jenny said. I popped the lasagna in the oven. "Okay, it'll be ready in an hour and a half" I said as we all went our separate ways.

    We all rushed into the kitchen when we heard the oven buzzer. "Alright, lasagna" Jay cheered. "Why did you guys get detention?" Kate asked Jenny. "We were talking while Kyle was giving a presentation in front of the class" she said. "How long until your play?" Shay asked Mike. "One month" he said. "You guys are lucky, you all got interests, I don't have any" I said. "Sure you do, you like to read" Cliff said as he started to laugh.

Chapter 2
The Journey Starts

I went to *The Black Cup* again. I needed somewhere quiet to do my homework and I was craving a coffee. I ordered a coffee and sat down in a booth looking out the window. I opened my books, got my pencil out and began to write. I looked up from my text book and saw a building next to *The Black Cup.* The people inside were dressed in black clothes and they wore different colored belts.

They were all facing one person and they were kicking and punching. I couldn't take my eyes off them, I was so enthralled, I wanted to learn more about it. I had to get my homework done, so I looked back down and tried to concentrate. Every couple minutes, I looked out the window. I didn't know why, but I felt like this was something that I wanted to do.

I finished my homework and my coffee as I kept staring out the window. Kara came over. "Can I get you anymore coffee?" she asked. "No thanks" I said as I continued to stare out the window. "What are you looking at?" she asked. "These people in black clothes, they look so intense, I would love to find out what they are doing" I said.

"It is called Kung Fu" she said. "Really?" I asked. "I've heard of that, but I don't know what it is" I said. "If you want I can take you over there when I'm off and show you around" she offered. "How would you show me around?" I asked. "Because, that is my father's Kung Fu school" she said. "Ya, I would love that" I said. "Okay, just wait until I'm off and we can go and I'll introduce you to my dad" she said as she walked away.

I opened up my notebook again and double checked my work. "Great, it all looks good" I congratulated myself. As I waited until Kara got off work, I watched them through the window. "Okay let's go" Kara said as she walked over to me. I got up and followed her out and across the street.

We walked in and sat on a bench at the back. There must have been close to one hundred people. We watched as they all punched and kicked in unison. Every time they made a movement, they would yell.

"That is my dad up there, he has been teaching at this school for forty five years. After everyone leaves, I'll introduce you" she said.

A while later they all bowed and started to leave. Once they all left, Kara and I walked up to her dad. "Kara, so good to see you" her dad said. "Dad, this is Ryan, he is interested in learning Kung Fu" she said. "Ah, so you want to learn Kung Fu do you? Why?" he asked. "I was intrigued when I saw that everyone looked so disciplined" I said. "Yes, Kung Fu teaches you discipline and strength" he said. "I can see that you are truly interested, perhaps there is hope for you" he said.

"My name is Ledger, come back tomorrow with Kara and I'll fit you in" he said. "Thank you sir, I am looking forward to it" I said as he smiled. "Bye daddy" Kara said as she kissed him on the cheek. We walked out of the building. "This will be fun" I said. "Ya, so meet me at *The Black Cup* tomorrow and after my shift we will go together" she said. "Have a good night" she said as she walked up the street. "You too" I yelled as I walked the opposite direction. All the way home I couldn't stop thinking about tomorrow.

"Why are you home so late?" Sally asked. I checked my watch, holy crap, I was late. "I'm sorry, I didn't know what time it was" I said. "You didn't answer my question" Sally said. "I was at *The Black Cup* and then I went out with a friend" I said. "Next time keep track of the time, it is passed your bedtime" she said as she kissed me on the forehead.

"I'm going to bed, goodnight, I love you" she said as she walked up the stairs. "I love you too" I said as I followed her upstairs and went to my room. I was so excited about tomorrow, I had a hard time falling asleep, but I finally managed to. I woke up before my alarm clock went off. I spent some time sitting and quieting myself and my mind. I went downstairs and into the kitchen where I saw everyone sitting at the table eating breakfast. I forgot what everyone was talking about, all I could think about was Ledger's Kung Fu school.

We left the house and started walking to school. Everyone was talking, except for me. "Are you okay Ryan?" Jenny asked. "What? Oh yes yes, I am fine, I am just thinking about something" I said. "What is it?" she asked intriguingly. "I met this girl who…" before I could finish, Shay cut me off. "A girl huh? Who is she?" she asked. "Her name is Kara" I said.

"Oh, you lucky guy" Jenny said. "it's not what you think, I told her I was interested in a club that she is in and she is going to show me around" I said. "Oh? What club?" Shay asked. "It's a Kung Fu club" I said. "Kung Fu? Isn't that with all the kicking and punching?" Jenny asked. "Ya, it is" I said. "She is going to show me around tonight and she just transferred to our school" I continued. "Wow, can we meet her?" Shay asked. "Sure" I said. "Do you like her?" Cutey asked. "Ya, I like her" I said.

The day went by really slow, I couldn't wait until the bell rang at the end of the day. I went to math class and saw Kara sitting in her desk already. "Hey" I said as I sat down. "Hey Ryan, how's it going?" she asked.

"Good, you?" I asked. "Good, I'm looking forward to tonight, my dad loves when we get new students" she said. "Ya, I'm excited too, I just can't stay too long because my mom freaked out on me last night" I said.

"Don't worry, a few times a week I get off work early" she said. Class was really boring, I was looking at the clock the whole time. It finally rang for lunch. "My brothers and sisters want to meet you. I told them about you and how your dad has a Kung Fu school" I said. "Okay" she said as we both walked into the lunch room. I saw them all sitting at the table by the window. "There they are" I said. "Wow, seven of them?" she asked. "I got five more that go to a different school" I said. "Wow, huge family" she said. "Yep" I replied.

We walked up to the table where they were eating. "Hey guys, this is Kara" I said as I introduced them all to her. "Ryan told me you transferred from another school, which school?" Cutey asked. "Widdletown High" she said. "Wow, I know some kids who go there, do you know Mark Himly?" Dream asked. "Ya, he goes to my dad's Kung Fu school" Kara said. "Do you know Sky Amber?" Dream asked. "Ya, he also goes to my dad's school" she said. "Do you also know Krim Toad?" he asked. "Yes, he also goes to my dad's school" she said.

After school, we walked home and in the front door and saw mom in the kitchen making supper. "What you making?" I asked. "Ribs and potatoes" she replied. "Mmmm" we all said as we rubbed our stomachs. A moment later we heard the bus pull up in front of the house. Cliff, Strong, Elizabeth, Kate and Rose walked in the front door in the middle of a heated argument.

"What's all this about?" Sally asked. "Cliff and Strong said we suck at the piano" Elizabeth said. "Well, they said we suck at basketball" Strong said. "That's enough you guys, you're both good at what you do" Sally said. "Mmm, do I smell ribs?" Cliff asked. "Ya, you do, they will be ready in forty five minutes" Sally said. We all ran to our rooms to start our homework. "I'll call you when supper is ready" Sally said.

"Supper" Sally yelled. We all came running into the kitchen and sat down at the table as she placed three racks of ribs in the center and a pot of potatoes. "Okay, dig in" she said. We all reached for the ribs first. "Here's some extra napkins because I know ribs can get a little messy" Sally said. "How was your day mom?" Cutey asked.

"It was nice and quiet for a change, I got to take an extra-long lunch, which I felt I deserved" Sally answered. "That's great mom" Kate said. "So, what started the argument between you guys?" Sally asked. "A girl that Strong likes from school asked him who sucks more, us at piano or them at basketball and he said that we were horrible" Kate said. Strong and I cleaned up the dishes after dinner was over.

"I am going to *The Black Cup*" I yelled as I was half way out the door. I walked in the door of *The Black Cup*, ordered myself a coffee and sat in the booth next to the window. I looked and looked but I didn't see Kara. About half an hour later, I saw her coming out from the back as I breathed a sigh of relief.

As she was taking customers' orders, she looked over at me and smiled. I smiled back and she turned back to the customers. There were less and less customers towards the time *The Black Cup* closed. Kara came up to me. "I just have to change and then we can go" she said. "Okay" I said. She came out a moment later. "Okay, let's go" she said. "Wow, you look beautiful" I said. "Thanks" she replied as we walked across the street.

We walked in to find that Ledger was in the middle of teaching a class so we sat on the benches at the back. He looked over and saw us. "Dan, can you run through what I was just doing with the class? I'll be right back" he said to one of the advance students. "Yes, of course" Dan replied as he stood facing the class. Ledger walked over to us. "It's good to see you my dear" he said as Kara kissed him on the cheek.

"Great to see you again Ryan, step into my office" he said as he pointed to a room in the corner. "Kara, you come too" he said as she followed. Kara and I sat in chairs facing his desk. "So, you are interested in learning Kung Fu" Ledger said. "Yes, I am" I said. "Tell me again why you want to learn?" he asked intently. "I saw great discipline and respect coming from your students and I like that kind of atmosphere" I said.

"Mmmm, I see I see" he said as he stroked his chin. "It looks like something that I really want to learn" I continued. "Well, if you're serious about it, I'll add you to the list of my students. I always love taking on new students, but I need students who are committed and willing to learn" he said. "Is that you?" he asked. "Yes sir" I said.

He got up from his chair. "Kara and I will show you around, introduce you to the class and we will come back here to talk some more" he said. He led the way as we both followed. "Can I have your attention for a moment class? This is Ryan and he is going to be starting here" he said. "Hello Ryan" the class said. "Dan, you can go back to teaching them" he said as he led us to the other side of the building which had a huge mat on the ground.

"This is where we spar, there are mirrors on the walls so we can see ourselves. There are staffs over there" he said as he pointed to the wall. He led us to the back, which also had a large mat. "This is where we use pads. We have kick pads and hand pads over there" he said as he pointed to the corner of the mat. "And where you see everyone standing, that is where we practice as a group" he said. "Well, that's the tour, come back to my office and we will talk more" he said as he led the way.

We sat back in the chairs. "So, I run classes every day, one in the morning and one in the evening. Kara is here for both of them, she is a senior instructor and helps the students who need it" he said. "I run beginner classes, intermediate classes and advanced classes and Kara also teaches all levels" he said. "In the mornings I like to do meditation for half of the class" he said.

"Do you like to meditate Ryan?" he asked. "Yes I do, I meditate quite often" I said. "Great, then if you want, you can come to the morning classes. I know you have school, but they are before school" he said. "Kara will tell you that I run a strict class, I expect respect, which means no talking. I want full concentration, full focus and participation" he said.

"The truth is that Kung Fu is not for everybody, it demands commitment and dedication. A lot of people end up quitting when it starts to get difficult. But if you stick with it, I'm sure you'll find it to be very rewarding" he said. "In saying that, your progress is totally up to you. If you don't put in the time and effort, you will never advance" he said. "I care a great deal about my students and one of my rules is, you have to get a part time job. This will show me that you have discipline" he said.

"Now, saying all that, do you have any questions for me?" he asked. "Is this more than just an external art?" I asked. "Yes, it is internal too, which means that it is a lifelong process of forming you into a different person. If that makes sense, you will see as you progress. It starts to change you, in every area of your life" he said. "Anything else?" he asked.

"What makes this school different from all the others" I asked. "Well, for one, like I said we focus on the inner development of the student as well as the external. We also adhere to a code of humility and honesty" he said. "Anything else" he asked. "No" I said. "Great" he said as he started to stand up. I want you to come back tomorrow with a signed note from your mom, allowing you to join my school" he said. "Okay, I will definitely get that note" I said. "Great, I'll see you tomorrow" he said as he pointed to the door.

"This is exciting, we will get to spend more time together" Kara said with excitement in her voice. "Ya, I am really looking forward to it" I said. "Do you want to walk home together?" I asked. "Actually, I am staying, I am going to help teach the class. But I will definitely see you tomorrow at class" she said. "Okay, bye" I said as I waved. "Bye" she said as she walked to the girls changing room.

"Okay, Kara is going to take over while I go attend to some important matters" Ledger said as he walked to his office. "Okay guys, pair up and do some slow speed sparring and I will come around and watch" she said. They went over to the sparring mat and started to spar together as Kara walked around and observed them. "Not so fast, slow it down" she said to Jim and Kim. She walked across the room.

"Keep your hands up Bob" she said as she noticed Bob dropping his hands. "Listen up everyone, focus on not dropping your hands when sparring" she said as she walked around. She glanced out the window and saw me looking in. She turned and kept on walking around her students. "I want everybody to have a seat on the mat" she said as they sat down. "Close your eyes and I want you to think about one technique that you are struggling with" she said as they started to think about it.

"Now I want you to imagine yourself doing the technique and performing it perfectly" she said. "Stand up and do the technique" she said as they stood up. "Now, I want you to stand there with your eyes closed and your knees bent and focus on your breathing. As you breathe in, feel the breath come in and energize you. And as you breathe out, feel it leave your body. "Open your eyes and bow and that will conclude this session" she said as they all started to walk to the changing rooms.

The doors opened and the students poured out of the building. "Well, how did I look?" Kara asked me. "You look very beautiful in your uniform" I said. "Really?" she asked. "Yes" I replied. "That is sweet of you to say" she said. "Can I walk you home" I asked. "No that's okay, my dad will give me a ride, but thanks for offering" she said as she turned and went back inside.

I felt so many emotions, I was excited about joining the school. I was attracted to Kara and I was excited that I found something that I was actually interested in. I didn't know if I should tell my family everything about what was happening. I guess they would find out eventually.

When I got home, my family were ready with questions. "Well, how did it go?" Mike asked. "It was awesome, I think I am really going to like this" I said. "Kara's dad showed me around the school and introduced me to his students" I continued. "Did you kiss Kara?" Cutey asked. "No, we are just friends" I said. "Sure you are" she said slyly. "Supper" mom yelled from the kitchen, we all came running in and sat down.

"Sweet, macaroni and cheese with hot dog pieces" Jay said as Sally put a huge pot in the center of the table. "So hunny, how did your thing go?" Sally asked. "Great, I can't wait to start" I said. "The teacher wants a signed note from you allowing me to join" I continued. "Sure, I'd be happy to write you a note" Sally said. "Ya and he even has a girlfriend" Shay said. "Is that true Ryan?" Sally asked. "No, she's just a friend" I said.

I walked into math class and sat down. I didn't see Kara there as the teacher began teaching. Half way through the class she rushed in, handed the teacher a late slip and headed for her seat. "Hi Ryan" she said. "Hey" I replied. "I slept in, I was up late doing homework" she said. "Good news, I got a note from my mom allowing me to join" I said. "That's great, you can give that to my dad and we can start training you" she said.

"Kara, stop talking" the teacher told her. "Sorry" she said. "We'll talk later" she said as she turned to the front. We walked to the lunch room together, I looked all over, but I couldn't see my brothers and sisters. "Huh, that's weird" I said as I looked at her. "I don't know where my family is" I continued. We both sat down. "How many years have you been training?" I asked. "Fifth teen years" she said. "Wow, that's awesome, you must be really good" I said. "I'm okay" she said.

She put her hands and elbows on the table and looked into my eyes. "So, what's your story?" she asked. "I was born here in Sweden, I am the youngest of my family. My mom raised us by herself because my dad died when I was seven" I said. "Oh god, that must have been horrible" she said. "Ya, it was rough, my dad and I were really close. After he died, I didn't talk to anyone for a month" I said.

"What about you?" I asked. "I was born in Shanghai. My dad and I moved here three years ago when my mom died" she said. "I feel your loss" I said. "My dad had a Kung Fu school in Shanghai, he let his brother take it over. And when we moved here, he opened up *The Dark Panther.* We ate the rest of our lunches and the bell rang.

"I'll see you at *The Black Cup* and we can go from there" she said. "Unless you want to walk home together" I said. "Well, my dad is going to pick me up, but let's walk home together tomorrow" she said. "Okay, sounds good" I said as I waved and went to my next class.

When the bell rang at the end of the day, I looked everywhere, but I couldn't find my family so I walked home by myself. When I walked in the door, I found them all at the kitchen table talking. "Why are you guys at home?" I asked. "Our teacher let us go to practice our play" Mike said. "Why are you guys at home?" I turned and asked Jenny. "Our teacher let us go to practice for our upcoming recital" Cutey said.

"It was lonely walking home all by myself" I said. "But I bet lunch time was great for you" Shay said. "Why do you say that?" I asked. "Because you got to be alone with Kara" Shay continued. "Owww" everyone said. "You guys are getting pretty close huh?" Elizabeth asked. "Ya, we are" I said. "Mom is working a double shift again tonight, so it is going to be a leftover night" Jay said. Jenny and Shay heated up the rest of the spaghetti while Elizabeth heated up the rest of the macaroni. After dinner I was out the door. "Have fun" everyone shouted.

When I walked into *The Black Cup*, Kara was just finishing up. "Order yourself a coffee, I will be a few more minutes" she said as I stood in line. I ordered a coffee, sat down and drank it while I waited. She got changed and came up to the booth that I was sitting at. "Okay, you ready?" she asked.

"Just about" I said as I chugged the last of my coffee. "Okay, now I am" I said. We walked across the street and into *The Dark Panther*. It was empty and Ledger was sitting at the front with his eyes closed. We both sat down with him and waited. "Where are the students?" Kara asked. "I told them to take a half an hour break" he said. "Did you get a note from your mom Ryan?" he asked.

"Yes, I did" I said as I pulled out the note from my pocket and handed it to him. "Great, I have a couple more things to go over with you before we can start. First, I tell all my students not to start fights outside of this school. Second, if and when someone asks you how good you are, I tell my students to respond by saying, I'm just okay.

If they hear that you are good, they might want to challenge you. And the final thing that I expect from my students is that they commit themselves to a journey of inner development" he said. "Now, is that something you can do?" he asked. "Yes, I can" I answered. "Great" he said as he got up and walked to his office. He came back a moment later with a black uniform. "This is your uniform, welcome to *The Dark Panther*" he said as he handed the uniform to me.

"We will begin as soon as my students come back" he said. "Go and change into your uniform and meet back here" he said as I walked into the change room. When I walked out of the change room, I found that all the students were standing, ready to learn. "I would like you all to welcome Ryan to the school" Ledger said. They all welcomed me, we then all turned to face Ledger and before I knew it, class was over.

"So, how did you like your first class?" Sky asked. "It was amazing, I learnt so much" I said. "Ya, isn't Ledger a good teacher?" he asked. "Ya, he really simplifies everything so we can understand it" I said. "See you next time" he said as he waved. "Okay, bye" I said as I went to the change room. As I was heading out I heard Kara behind me.

"Wait for me, I'll walk with you, I told my dad that I don't need a ride" she said. We started to walk to Kara's house. "So, what did you think of your first class?" she asked. "I really liked it, I can tell that your dad has a real passion for Kung Fu" I said. "Ya, he loves it, he eats and breathes this stuff" she replied. "Did you finish that math homework that we got today?" she asked.

"Ya, I did it when I got home" I said. "I am having some problems with it, it is hard" she said. "Can you help me?" she asked. "Ya, I will help you, it is not due for a few days. I can come to *The Black Cup* earlier and help you, if it's not too crazy busy. "That might work, but if not, you can come over to my house after Kung Fu and help me" she said. "Sure" I replied. "Great" she said as she grabbed my upper arm and rested her head on it as we walked.

"This is my house on the right" she said. "Thanks for walking me home" she said as she kissed me on the cheek. "You're welcome, I'll see you tomorrow at school, goodnight" I said as I waved. As I started to walk back, I started to smile as I thought about her. It started to get cold so I rubbed my arms to try to warm myself up, since I didn't have a jacket on.

I walked in the front door but I didn't hear anybody. I looked at the clock. Wow, it was late, I better get to bed, I thought to myself. I ran upstairs and got in bed, I thought about Kung Fu and Kara as I closed my eyes. I woke up to the sound of laughing. I walked downstairs and found everyone at the table eating waffles. "Morning, is there any waffles left?" I asked. "Ya, there are a few more" Cutey said.

I popped some on a plate and sat down at the table. "Why were you so late coming home?" Shay asked. "I walked Kara to her house" I said. "We got our play almost perfect" Mike said. "You should watch it, it is even better than last time you saw it" Jay said. "Ya, okay I will" I replied. "How is your piano practicing going?" I asked. "Good, good, we are getting confident" Shay said.

As we were leaving the house, we saw mom pull up in her mini cooper. She got out and walked toward us. "I'm glad I caught you guys before you left, I am going to be working late again tonight. I will be gone before you get home. Sorry that I am working so much, I promise we will all do something fun when my work calms down" she said as she kissed us on the forehead and went in the front door.

We waited with Elizabeth, Cliff, Strong, Kate and Rose at the bus stop until the bus came and then we walked to school. When we got to school, I saw Kara sitting on the steps outside the front door. "Go talk to her" Jenny said as she nudged me. I walked up to her.

"Hey, you okay?" I asked as I sat down beside her. I could see that she was crying. "My aunty called last night, my uncle died yesterday" she said as she sobbed. "Oh god, I am so sorry" I said as I put my arm around her. "My dad is all choked up about it, they were very close" she said.

The bell rang as we both stood up. "I'll walk you to class, okay" I said. "Okay" she said as we both walked in the front door. I watched as she went into her classroom and I started walking to mine. I saw Easter, the bully, walking towards me. "Where are you going jerk?" he asked as he punched me in the stomach. I fell to the ground and I heard him laughing as he continued to walk by. I managed to pick myself up a few minutes later. He is going to get what's coming to him one day, I thought.

"I have a great idea" Kara said at the lunch room table. "What is it?" I asked. "You should get a job at *The Black Cup* with me. "My manager is looking for some more people" she said. "Ya, that sounds like a great idea" I said. "I'll introduce you to him when you get there" she said. "Get where?" Dish asked as they all came and sat with Kara and me.

"I am going to get a job at *The Black Cup,* where Kara works" I said. "Why would you want a part time job?" Jenny asked. "One of the requirements of this Kung Fu school is to get a job, it teaches us discipline"

Kara replied. "Our little brother is growing up" Dream said as he tousled my hair as I hit his hand away.

"Knock it off" I said. "You should come and watch our play Kara" Mike said. "It is in a couple of weeks" he continued. "Sure, I would love to" she said. The bell rang and we all went to our classes. Kara walked with me to my class. "I'll see you after school" she said as she kissed me on the cheek. "Alright, bye" I said as she turned and walked down the hall.

Right before I walked in, I saw Jenny out of the corner of my eye. She was sitting in front of her locker as I walked over to her. "What's wrong?" I asked. "Easter called me an ugly piece of crap" she said. "What?" I asked. "That asshole" I continued. "Don't listen to him, you are beautiful" I said. "Really?" she asked. "Of course you are" I said. "Thanks Ryan" she said as she stood to her feet and gave me a kiss on the cheek.

At the end of the day, I walked out the front doors and I saw Kara waiting for me. "Hi Kara" I said. "How was the rest of your day?" I asked. "It was boring, how was yours?" she asked. "It was okay" I said. "After you walked me to class, I saw Jenny. She was upset because Easter called her an ugly piece of crap" I said.

"That guy is stupid, I wish I could kick his ass" she said. On the way to my house we passed *The Black Cup*. "Let's go talk to the manager now, before it gets too busy" she said. "Okay" I said as we walked in. "Roy, this is Ryan, he would like a part time job here" Kara said. "Great, I need more people, do you have any experience serving coffee?" he asked. "No, but I like to drink it" I answered.

"Good enough, fill out this application and hand it to me when you're done" he said as he handed me a piece of paper. A few moments later I returned it to him and he looked it over. "Great, you can start tomorrow, I will have a uniform ready for you" he said. "See you in a little bit Kara" he said. "Thank you" I said as we walked out and headed to my house.

"So I'll see you later" she said as she hugged me. I walked inside to find everyone watching television. "Mom left us money for dinner, so we can get whatever we want" Jay said. "We were thinking pizza, what do you think?" Cutey asked. "Ya, pizza is good" I said as I went upstairs to my room. "Pizza is on its way" Shay yelled to me twenty minutes later.

The doorbell rang, Shay gave the delivery man the money and took the pizzas into the kitchen. "Pizza is here" she yelled as everyone dashed into the kitchen. "Awesome, I'm starving" Jenny said. "Me too" I replied. "I might be late again tonight" I said as I took a bite. "Out with your girlfriend?" Cutey asked facetiously, but I didn't respond. After supper I ran upstairs to do my homework. I wanted to finish it all before I left for the night.

Chapter 3
Serious Training

Kara and I walked into *The Dark Panther* together and we went to our change rooms. We came out and sat on the floor and waited for the other students to arrive. Ledger walked out of his office and walked to the front. "Good evening everyone, I trust you had a good day" he said. He started to walk around us in a circle.

"Tonight we will be focusing on standing your ground. No matter what happens in a fight, no matter how badly you get hurt, never drop your cover hands. As long as you have your hands up, you have a chance. The minute you drop your hands, your opponent will rip you apart. If you get knocked to the ground, don't just lay there while your opponent kicks you, get yourself up" he said.

"Let's go over to the mat and split into pairs" he continued. "I will be your partner" Kara said as she looked at me. "I want one person to push the other down and rush him. I want you to get up right away, ready to fight" he said. Kara pushed me, I fell to the mat as she started to rush me. I quickly got to my feet with my hands in front of my body. "Good job Ryan" Ledger congratulated me.

"Now switch positions" he said. I pushed Kara, she fell on the mat and I started to rush her. She immediately got up with her hands ready to fight. "Great job everyone" Ledger said. "Now this time I want you to be more aggressive" he continued. Kara shoved me down to the mat, rushed me and pretended to kick me. I moved out of the way of her foot and stood up with my hands ready to fight.

"Good effort guys" Ledger said. It was my turn to shove Kara down. She dropped to the mat, I rushed at her and pretended to kick her. She moved out of the way as she stood up with her hands ready to attack me. "Very good" he said. We practiced that over and over, for half the class. "Alright guys, come back to the middle" Ledger said.

"We train to never give up and never give in. The moment we give up the fight, our opponent could hurt us or worse, kill us" he said. "This will build up your mental strength and spill over into every area of your life. You will start to see that you don't give up as easily on things that you used to" he said. He grabbed Kara to show us again. He pushed her down and Ledger rushed into her with a kick.

She avoided the kick and quickly stood up with her hands ready. "If you don't bring your hands up, you won't have time to defend and your opponent will be all over you" he said. "Watch" he said as Kara kept her hands down and they did the same thing. This time when Kara got up, she didn't have her hands up. Ledger rushed her and pretended to punch her. "This is what will happen" he said. "Everyone take a seat" he said as we all sat down on the floor. "Close your eyes and run through in your minds what you just did" he said. "This will help you to achieve accuracy in your moves.

"That's it for tonight, I'll see you all here tomorrow morning at six thirty for meditation" Ledger said. We all went to the change rooms. I walked Kara home and this time she kissed me on the lips. "Goodnight Ryan, I'll see you tomorrow morning" she said as she unlocked her door and went inside.

I was walking through a cross walk when a car came out of nowhere and zipped around the corner nearly hitting me. Holy crap, that was close, I thought as I continued to walk home. I unlocked the door and heard silence. Everyone was in bed as I looked at the clock. "Wow, eleven" I whispered. I tiptoed upstairs and went to my room.

I was the first one up the next morning. I got dressed and quietly went downstairs. I had some breakfast and walked to *The Dark Panther*. From down the street I saw Kara. She was waiting outside the front door for me. "Good morning Ryan" she said. "Morning" I replied. We went inside, got changed and sat with the other students on the sparring mat. Ledger walked up to the front of the class and sat down with his legs crossed.

"I want you all to sit like me and put your arms on your knees with your palms facing up. Close your eyes and clear your mind of everything. This may take longer for some people, but if you keep at it, you will eventually get there. If you are having trouble, focus on your breathing. By doing this, you are not able to think of anything else" he said.

"When you reach that place where your mind is clear, then and only then can you listen to yourself. This will get you in touch with who you are. It will get you in touch with what emotions you are feeling and it sets a positive mood for your day" he continued.

We all sat there for half an hour, until some students started to get restless. "Now open your eyes" he said as we all opened our eyes. "How do you feel?" he asked. We started to shout out answers. "Calm" one student said. "Relaxed" another student said. "Centered" another student said. "At peace" another student said.

"When you connect with yourself and find out who you are, you will understand yourself and the world around you. Meditation is important, because the body and mind talk to you. Unless you are listening, you won't hear what it has to say. Many people go through their lives without understanding who they are and what they are capable of" he said. "That is it for this morning, I look forward to seeing you all here tonight" he said as we all left to get changed.

As Kara and I were walking to school, we saw my family in the distance. "Is that my family?" I asked. "I think it is" I answered myself. We ran up behind them. "Morning guys" I said. "Morning Ryan, where were you?" Jenny asked. "We went to morning class, Kara's dad runs a meditation class in the mornings" I said.

"Mom left another note, she is working another double shift" Jay said. "We were thinking of making tacos, what do you think" Shay asked. "Ya, that sounds good" I said. "We are going to the store to pick up some meat after school, you coming?" Dream asked. "No, I'm going to walk Kara home" I said.

"You're welcome to come for dinner Kara" Cutey said. "Thanks, but I will be working" she said. "Oh ya, I forgot to tell you guys that I got a job with Kara, so I won't be home for supper" I said. "Ya, you forgot to mention that to us" Jay said. "Ya, it just slipped my mind" I said.

Kara and I were walking to math class, when I saw Easter coming towards us. "Is this your girlfriend jerk?" he asked as he reached out to grab me by the throat. Kara took his hand and wrapped it around his back and kicked him as he dropped to his knees. "That is enough from you" she said in a threatening voice.

He got up from the floor. "I'll see you when your girlfriend's not around" he said as he walked by. "I would just like to kick that guy's ass" I said as I looked at her. "Thank you for doing something" I said. "You'll learn defense techniques like that eventually" she said as we walked into math class and sat down.

At the end of the day I walked her home. "You have time for a quick bite to eat, before you have to be at work. You should go home and eat with your family" she said. I ran home as I looked back and waved to her. "What are you doing here? I thought you were working" Dream said. "I still am, I have a few minutes so I thought I would come home and eat with you guys" I said as I sat down.

I grabbed a taco, loaded it up and bit into it. "Good huh?" Cutey asked. "Ya, really good" I said. "What are you guys up to tonight?" I asked. "We are going to a movie" Dream said. "Well, have fun, I am off to my first day of work" I said as I walked to the front door. "Bye Ryan" Shay said as they all waved at me.

"Here is your uniform" Roy said as he handed me a red shirt and black pants. "There is a change room in the back and don't forget to wear a hair net" he continued. "Since today is your first day, I just want you to shadow Kara and the others. Whatever they need, you can help them" he said. "Got it" I said.

I was lucky that it wasn't too busy, only a handful of people came in. I wiped the tables off when the customers left. I swept up around the booths and I cleaned the bathrooms. "Since it's not busy right now Kara, why don't you show Ryan how the coffee machines work?" Roy asked Kara. "Okay" she said as she ran through how the espresso machine worked. She showed me how the hot chocolate machine worked and how the iced coffee machine worked.

"How did you like your first day?" Kara asked. "It was fun" I answered. "Thanks for your help Ryan" Roy said as Kara and I walked out the door. We walked into *The Dark Panther*, got changed and stood, ready to learn. "Kara, can I see you in my office please?" Ledger asked as Kara walked to his office. "I want you to take Ryan aside and teach him stances while I continue with the rest of the class" he said.

"Okay, I will" she said as she walked up to me. "Come over here Ryan, I want to show you stances" she said as she led me to the corner. "Stand with your feet slightly apart" she said. "This is called a neutral stance. "I'm going to show you what is called a left fighting stance. Keep your left foot forward and drop your right foot back, but on an angle with your toes facing right, like this" she said as she showed me.

"Now you try" she said. "Good, good, you got the idea" she said. "Now the other stance is called a right fighting stance. You keep your right foot forward and you drop your left foot back, but also on an angle with your toes pointed left, like this" she said as she showed me. "Now that you got the idea, we will work on it until it becomes natural for you" she said.

We stood in the corner and worked on stances until Ledger called us back half an hour later. We rejoined the other students. They were punching from a right fighting stance. "So, remember what I told you about right fighting stances? Now just punch from this stance. And when you do, you're going to roll your hips as you punch, like this" she said as she demonstrated it for me.

"That's it, you got it" she said as we continued to punch. "Okay, now from the left fighting stance" Ledger said as we all switched our footing positions. It was a little hard for me, because I am right handed. "Concentrate, make your punches straight"

Ledger said as he walked around to me. "Alright, come back to a neutral stance. That is it for tonight, great job everyone. Rest up and I'll see you all here tomorrow night" he said as he walked to his office. We poured into the change rooms, got changed and then poured out.

We walked to Kara's front step. "When you have time, I want you to practice those stances" she said as she kissed me on the lips. I started walking home thinking how awesome Kung Fu was. I walked in the front door and everyone was in the kitchen talking about the movie. "How was the movie guys?" I asked.

"It was so good, you should go see it" Dream said. "Ya Ryan, there was so much action in it" Dish said. "How was your first night at work?" Elizabeth asked. "It was fun, I got to meet a lot of new people" I said. "I am going to bed, I am exhausted" I said as I went upstairs. "Goodnight" everyone shouted.

"Goodnight" I shouted back. The phone rang a while later. "Hello" Cutey said. "Hi Cutey, it's Kara, can I talk to Ryan?" she asked. "Ya sure, one second" she said. "Ryan, telephone, it's Kara" she yelled up the stairs. "Hi Kara" I said. "Hey Ryan, I still need help with that homework, can you come over tomorrow and help me?" she asked. "Oh ya, I totally forgot about that, I'll be over tomorrow" I said. "Thanks, I have to go, goodnight" she said. "Goodnight" I said as I hung up the phone.

    The next morning, I meditated by myself in my room before I went downstairs. "Hopefully mom will be home tonight" Kate said. "Ya, it's been a while since we've seen her" Jenny said. Not a moment after she said that, Sally walked in the door. Jenny ran up to her and gave her a hug. "I've missed you" she said. "I've missed you guys too and as far as I know, I am off tonight, unless they call me in with an emergency" Sally said.

    The bus pulled up to the house. "The bus is here" Shay yelled. Cliff, Strong, Elizabeth, Rose and Kate rushed out the door and onto the bus. We walked out the door next, after saying goodbye to Sally. Everybody was talking about the movie the whole way to school.

We got to school and went our separate ways. I was walking to class when Easter came up behind me. "Looks like your girlfriend isn't here to save you" he said. He pushed me down and I remembered what Ledger taught me about always being ready. I immediately stood up and put my hands up in a cover position. I looked at him with intensity and for whatever reason, he walked away.

I don't know if I scared him or if he was board. But whatever the reason, he went away. I felt a rush of confidence pour over me like a flood. It was a great feeling. I walked into class with my head held high. Everyone said hi to me, which was unusual because normally I was invisible to them.

"What happened to Easter? I just saw him walk past me and he didn't even try to do anything" Kara asked. "I stood up to him and he pushed me to the ground. I got up, put my hands in front of me, looked intensely into his eyes and he ran off" I said proudly. "Wow, good job, it's about time someone stood up to that jerk" she said.

"Take out your books and read pages seventy two through seventy nine and answer the questions on page eighty. They are to be put on my desk on your way out" the teacher said. It took us all class to do them. When the bell rang, we put our completed questions on his desk on the way out.

On our way to the lunch room, we saw Easter coming towards us with one other guy. I turned to Kara. "Uh oh" I said. "Run" she said as we ran in the opposite direction. We hid in the girl's bathroom around the corner as they ran by. We waited a while until we were certain they were gone and then we came out.

"I am pretty sure I could have taken them, but we are taught not to engage in fights" Kara said. We saw my brothers and sisters sitting at a table in the lunch room and joined them. "So, tomorrow we are practicing our play during lunch, you guys should come watch" Dream said. "Ya, we will be there" Kara said.

I walked Kara to her front door. "See you at work" she said. I got home, walked in the door and saw Sally sitting in the kitchen. "Mom, great that you're home, we can have supper together" I said. "Smells good, what are we having?" Kate asked. "We are having casserole and green beans" Sally said. Strong and I started to set the table.

"Supper" Sally shouted as we all sat down at the table and started to heap spoonfuls onto our plates. "What has been going on around here?" Sally asked. "Just a lot of practicing our activities" Elizabeth said. "How is the job going Ryan?" Sally asked. "It's good, I am really liking it" I said. "That's good and what about the Kung Fu" she asked. "I absolutely love it, I can't get enough of it" I said. "That's great, I am glad that you finally found something that you enjoy and are passionate about" she said.

"Well, work has been so busy for me, I tell ya, I could sleep for a week" Sally said. "Ya, you look tired" Jenny said. "Oh yes, I am" she replied. "I am glad I am home, I missed you guys like crazy" she said. "I hope you ate other things than just pizza" she said. "Ya we did" Dream said. We finished dinner and all got up.

"Here mom, let me and Dream do the dishes for you, you go relax in a bath" I said. "Thank you dear" she said as she walked up stairs and turned on the water. I loaded the last plate in the dishwasher and turned to Dream. "Well, I got to go to work, I'll see you later" I said as I headed to the door and put on my shoes.

I got to *The Black Cup* and changed into my uniform. When I walked out of the back, I saw a line up at the counter. I started helping customers on an empty till. Kara was on the till right beside me. We helped each other with each other's orders. The shift passed by so fast. It was so busy and before we knew it, we were getting changed to go home.

"Great job tonight everybody, we served a lot of customers" Roy said as we all walked out. We walked in *The Dark Panther*, got changed and stood ready to learn. Ledger walked in, he didn't even say hi, he just went straight into teaching. "Close your eyes and be conscious of what's around you" he said. "Where am I now?" he asked as he started circling the students.

He asked certain students. "Bob, where am I?" he asked. "You are behind us" he said. "That's right" Ledger said. He was silent for a few moments. "Mark, where am I?" he asked. "You are at the front" Mark said. "Wrong, I am on your right" he said. A few more minutes passed. "Ryan, where am I?" he asked. "You are at the back" I said. "Correct" he said.

"Sky, where am I?" he asked. "You are in front" Sky answered. "Wrong, I am on your left" he said. "Okay, open your eyes, now the purpose of this exercise was to make you aware of what is around you. No matter what you are up against or who you are fighting, you must be aware of everything at all times. Even walking down the sidewalk, you must be aware of your surroundings. Because you never know what could happen. You could end up hurt or even dead if you are not always on the lookout" he said.

"Okay, let's run through this again" he said. He walked up to me and whispered. "You're going to be the second person walking around" he said. He walked one way and I walked the other. "Kara, where am I?"

Ledger asked. "You're at the front" she said. "Very good" he said. Ledger stood in front of a student and I stood behind the student. "Kim, where am I?" I asked. "You're in front" she said. "Wrong, I am behind you" I said.

"Now, let's lay on the floor and we are going to run through the same drill" Ledger said as we all laid on the floor. "Jim, where am I?" he asked. "You are at the front" Jim said. "Wrong, I am at your left" Ledger said. "Kim, where am I?" he asked. "You are at the back" she said. "Wrong, I am at the front" he said. "Kirm, where am I?" he asked. "You are at my left" he said. "Wrong, I am at your right" he said.

"Open your eyes and stand up, you see how difficult it is lying down? See how something so miner as lying down can cause your mind to get confused?" he asked. "Once you master your awareness, it will be near impossible to surprise you" Ledger said.

"Tomorrow morning we will have meditation again, so if you can make it, that will be great" he said. "Great work tonight guys" he said. "I want you to work on your awareness. Sit in your yard and just listen to the sounds around you and try to identify where they are and what they are" he said. We all went into the change rooms and walked out of the building.

"That was an awesome class tonight" I said to Kara as I walked her home. "Ya, I love doing drills like that, it really puts you in tune with yourself and the things around you" she said as we got to her front door. I followed her in and up to her room to help her with the homework that was due the next day. She pulled out her books and notebook and we got to work.

"Okay, now this question I almost got, but I think something is wrong with the answer" she said. "Ya, here is what you did wrong" I said as I took the eraser, erased the last part of the equation and put in two different numbers. "You almost had it, you were just off a bit" I said. "Now, this one I couldn't get at all" she said.

"The formula is on this page" I said as I flipped to page fifty two. "Read this" I said as I handed her the book. I waited until she was done reading. "Oh, I think I got it" she said as she started to write the equation. "How's this?" she asked as she showed me. "Perfect, that is exactly right" I said.

I coached her through ten more problems. Before I left I turned to her. "Do you want to do a little Kung Fu before I leave?" I asked. "Sure" she said. We both stood in a right fighting stance. "Let's do ten punches and slide step into a left fighting stance and do ten more punches" she said. "Ready?" she asked. "Ya" I replied.

After we did that, she got me to sit and close my eyes as she walked around me. "Where am I?" she asked. "You're behind me" I said. "Very good" she said. She walked a bit more. "Where am I?" she asked. "You're to the right of me" I said. "Very good Ryan" she said. "I think you got that drill down pat" she said. "Well, it's late, I should go" I said as I stood up.

"Goodnight" I said. "I'll walk you to the door" she said. We walked outside. "Have a goodnight" I said. She leaned in to kiss me and I kissed her back. We kissed for a few moments and then I turned and walked down the steps. "See you in the morning" she said.

Chapter 4
This Time It's Personal

I walked into *The Dark Panther* to find everyone there. I quickly got changed and I quietly sat down. "Let all your worries go, let everything go and just be here in the moment. Listen to what your mind and body is telling you, they will never steer you wrong" Ledger said. Towards the end of class, we heard a loud bang and everyone opened their eyes.

Suddenly, the door flew open and Easter and his gang surrounded us. We immediately sprang to our feet and threw our hands in the cover position. Easter and his gang took out their knives and got ready to attack. "Quick, form a tight circle" Ledger said to the beginner students. His advanced students and him formed a larger circle to protect them.

Ledger threw a kick that hit Easter right in the face and he fell to the ground. He got up a few moments later and wiped the blood from his mouth. He looked at his gang and gave the signal for them to attack. One of his men took a slash at Kara, she moved back and stepped forward with a straight right punch to the throat, dropping him to the ground.

A few of Easter's gang went for the beginner students and stabbed Kim, Mark and Sky. They dropped to the ground motionless. Ledger rushed up to them and took them out one by one. He smacked one in the head with his right elbow and floored him with a left punch to the side of the throat. He swept another one's foot and drove his right elbow into his chest, causing him to spit up blood.

He went up to the last guy and thrusted his elbow straight up on his chin. His head flew backwards as Ledger threw a left punch and a right punch at his throat. Easter saw that they were no match for them and signaled for the rest of his gang to leave. They ran out the door, leaving behind a few that were dead on the ground.

"Is everyone okay?" Ledger asked. The beginner students were still in shock. "Is anyone hurt?" Kara asked. "No, we're fine" we all said as we looked at Mark, Kim, and Sky's bodies which were motionless on the ground. "Instead of having class tonight, we are going to hold a memorial service for them in the backyard" Ledger said.

"This horrific act shouldn't have happened, we must assume that they will come back and we must be ready for them" he said. "I know it will be hard to focus on what you have to do today, but try your best" Ledger said. We all got changed and went about our day. Kara waited for me at the door and we started to walk to school.

"When my mom finds out what happened, she is going to pull me out of *The Dark Panther*" I said. "Don't tell her" Kara said. "She will find out eventually" I replied. "You never know, maybe not" she said. "What if we see Easter at school?" Kara asked. "I guess we will just wait and see what happens" I said. "We can't show fear, that is what he wants to see from us, we must stand up to him" I continued. "You're right" she said as we walked to math class, luckily we didn't see him.

"Everyone hand in the assignment I gave you a few days ago" the teacher said. We all got up, put the assignment on his desk and sat back down. I couldn't concentrate on what the teacher was saying, I was still shaken up from this morning. Kara looked over at me and could see that I was upset. "I know it's hard to make sense of all this, but you are doing great" she whispered.

The bell rang for lunch and everybody rushed out the door. We got to the lunch room and sat down at a table by the window. "Still no sign of Easter and his gang" I said. "How come you're handling this so well?" I asked. "I have seen this before" she said. "Where?" I asked.

"Back in my country, the mafia would come to the Kung Fu schools and demand a percentage of the money. If we didn't give them a percentage, they would kill all the students and even the master" she said. "One day they came into the school that my dad was running at the time. They killed all his students, we were the only two left alive and the next day we left the country" she continued.

At the end of the day, I waited for Kara outside the front door. "I am going to walk home by myself, I need to be alone and try to absorb what happened" I said. "Okay, I'll see you at work" she said as she kissed me on the cheek. We both walked in separate directions. I had a feeling that someone was following me so I started to run as fast as I could.

I made it home, locked the door and looked out the window to see if I could see anyone. I couldn't see anyone, maybe I was just being paranoid. "What are you looking at?" a voice came from the kitchen, it was my mom. "Just checking to see if the others are coming" I lied. I walked into the kitchen and sat down. "I am off again tonight, so I thought we could go out for dinner, we'll leave early so you won't miss any work" she said.

The front door opened and everyone came rushing in. "Leave your shoes on, we're going out to eat" Sally said. "You off tonight?" Shay asked. "Yes I am" Sally replied. We took Sally's car, Shay's car and

Cutey's car. We went to our favorite restaurant, *The Hungry Man*.

I kept having the feeling that we were being watched. I then saw someone who looked like Easter in the bushes. I didn't know if I was seeing things or if he was actually there. I ignored what I saw and went back to laughing and talking with my family, but every once in a while I glanced out the window.

On the way back, Shay dropped me off in front of *The Black Cup*. "Thanks" I said as I opened the car door and ran inside. Work went by very slowly because there were not many customers. I found myself staring at the clock. "What's wrong?" Kara asked. She could see in my face that I was scared.

"Maybe I'm just paranoid, but I think Easter is following me. I felt someone follow me home and then when I went out for dinner with my family, I saw someone out the window" I said. "You're probably just imagining it" she said. "Ya, maybe your right" I said as I went to wipe off the tables. We closed up and walked to *The Dark Panther*.

"Let's go out back" Ledger said as we all followed him. As we got to the back, we saw three caskets side by side and three holes in the ground next to the caskets. We all stood around the caskets in a circle as Ledger walked up to the caskets. "It's a sad day when a master's students are taken from him. We now bestow upon them the title of master, seeing that there training is over" he said as he bowed his head.

Kara walked up beside Ledger. "They were not just our students, they were also our friends, and we will miss them" she said. We all bowed our heads as a few of us lowered the caskets into the holes and piled dirt on top. "Let's have a moment of silence for our lost brothers and sisters" Ledger said. Silence filled the air for a few moments. "We will not have morning meditation tomorrow so come back tomorrow evening" Ledger said.

I turned to leave and I heard gun shots. I turned around to find four students on the ground with blood dripping from their heads. "Everyone get down" I shouted as we all crawled back inside *The Dark Panther*. I didn't know for certain, but I assumed that the shooter was Easter. Ledger stumbled in a moment later. "Oh my god, you've been shot" Kara cried. "It's not that bad" Ledger said.

"Ryan, come help me" Kara said as I rushed over. "I saw a first aid kit in his office" I said as we carried him into his office. We put him on the table and ripped off his shirt. He was shot in the right arm. "Get me some alcohol and a knife" I said to Kara. She searched his desk drawers and handed me some alcohol and a knife. I poured alcohol on his wound.

"Here bite on this" I said as I gave him a cloth. I stuck the knife in his skin and popped out the bullet. I poured some more alcohol on his wound. "There, you're going to be just fine" I said. "Thanks" he said as he put his hand on my shoulder. We walked out of the office and found the students pacing back and forth. "In light of the circumstances, we are going to take a few days off" Ledger said.

I walked Kara home. "Come on" she said as she took my hand and we went upstairs to an empty room. She spend four hours teaching me techniques. She showed me how to be both defensive and offensive. She taught me how to use my opponent's body weight against him. She taught me holds and how to flip my opponent.

"The most important thing to remember is, don't think, just react" she said. "Flow with your opponent, feel his energy. The more relaxed you are, the faster you will be and the more power you will generate" she continued. Once she saw that I was exhausted, we stopped. We went down to the kitchen and she got out two bottles of water from the fridge. "Great job" she said as she smiled at me.

Ledger was working in his office, when he heard a loud bang coming from the front door. He looked out from the door way of his office. The front door flew open as Easter and his gang rushed inside. Ledger ran to his sword cabinet and pulled out his Katana. He walked into the room where Easter and his gang were. Ledger raised up his Katana as Easter's gang circled him.

One guy rushed towards Ledger and Ledger slashed him on the neck as he dropped to the ground and his head rolled away. Another guy slipped a kick in and hit Ledger in the stomach, sending him flying to the ground. Ledger quickly stood to his feet and thrusted his sword into the guy's chest and he crumbled to the ground.

Another guy punched him in the face as Easter snuck up behind him and stabbed him in the back with a knife. Ledger dropped to the ground as he grabbed Easter by the arm. "You don't remember me, but I remember you and you know my father, the mafia boss" he said as Ledger went motionless. Easter and his gang ransacked the place and then left.

Kara walked me home, on the way we decide to stop off at *The Dark Panther*, to talk to Ledger. We walked in to find the place trashed. We saw Ledger lying in the middle of the floor as Kara ran over to him. "Dad, dad" she yelled. Ledger struggled for breath. "Who did this?" she asked. "The son of the mafia boss from China" Ledger said as he took his final breath.

"Noooo" she screamed. "Come on, we should go, it's not safe here" I said as we walked out. I took her back to her house. I made her something to eat, but she refuse to eat it. She cried all night long. I decided to stay with her, to try to console her. I brought her to her room and laid her on her bed. I started to leave. "Can you stay with me for a while? Just until I fall asleep" she said. "Of course" I said as I laid beside her. She stopped crying an hour later and fell asleep. I went downstairs and fell asleep in the spare bedroom.

The next morning, I went upstairs to check on her. "What are you doing?" I asked as I saw her packing her bag. "I am going to China" she said. "What? Why?" I asked. "I am going to stop this once and for all" she said. "We'll just take care of Easter and his gang and that will be the end of it" I said. "You don't understand how this guy operates. Easter and his gang are just the beginning. He will keep sending men, until we are dead, I must end it" she said.

"Then I am coming with you" I said. "You can't, what about your family?" she asked. "I'll tell my mom that we are going on a weeklong training event. She'll let me because it is spring break anyhow. Besides, I can help you, it's personal now" I said. "Okay" she said. "Call your mom and then we'll head to the airport" she said.

We drove her car to the airport and checked with the flight attendant to see when the next flight to Shanghai was. "Next flight is leaving at three this afternoon" the flight attendant said. We had breakfast and then waited in the waiting area. We quickly had lunch and then boarded the plane. "Your flight to Shanghai will be eleven hours, welcome aboard and I hope you enjoy your flight" the voice on the intercom said.

Kara slept on my shoulder until the flight attendant came over to us. "What would you like for supper? We have steak and potatoes, fish and vegetables or soup and a sandwich" she said. "I will have the steak and potatoes" I said. "And I will have the fish and vegetables" Kara said. "Okay, great" the flight attendant said as she wrote it down.

"And what do you want to drink?" she asked. "Two waters please" I said. "Coming right up" she said as she went to the next passenger. She came back twenty minutes later and placed two plates in front of us. "There you are, enjoy" she said. "Thank you" I said as we started to eat. "So, how will we find this guy?" I asked as I took a bite. "He owns a night club that he likes to hang out at" she said. "How do you know that?" I asked. "My dad hired a private detective to follow him" she said.

The plane landed at the Shanghai airport. "Thank you for choosing *China Air*, enjoy your stay in China" the voice said over the intercom. We walked out the front door of the airport and got in a cab. "Thirty Two Zing Drive" Kara told the driver. "I have a house here where we can stay" she said. The cab pulled up in front of Kara's house. She handed the driver some money and we went inside.

"Make yourself comfortable" she said as she went to her room to change. I walked in a room and saw twenty swords hanging on the wall. "Wow, are these yours?" I asked.

"Ya, me and my dad used to use them for training" she said. "Come with me, I want you to meet a friend of mine, she's a student of my dad's friend" she said. "Okay" I said as I grabbed my coat and followed her.

We walked down the street for about twenty minutes, until we came to a brown building. "This is it" she said as we walked up and she pushed the intercom for apartment three. "Hello?" a voice on the intercom asked. "Hi Nancy, its Kara, how are you?" she asked. "Hi girl, I'm good, come on up" she said as she buzzed us in.

We walked in and down the hall. She was standing in the doorway with her arms open. They hugged each other. "It's great to see you Nancy" Kara said. "You too Kara" Nancy replied. "This is Ryan, he is from Sweden" she said. "It's nice to meet you Ryan" Nancy said. "You too Nancy" I said. "Please come in you two" Nancy said as we walked in to the living room and sat down.

"Can I get you guys anything to drink?" she asked. "Sure, I'll have a water" I said. "Me too please" Kara said. She left and came back with two waters. "How long has it been

Kara?" Nancy asked. "It's got to be three years or longer" Kara replied. "What brings you back here?" Nancy asked.

"My dad was murdered by the mafia boss's son. We have come to put an end to it, before he kills us" Kara said. "Oh Kara, I am so sorry to hear about your dad" Nancy said as she put her hand on Kara's leg.

"What can I do to help?" she asked. "We are going to his night club to talk to him and we could use some backup" Kara said. "Sure, I'll come and help you out" Nancy said. "It's going to be dangerous" Kara said. "Then we better be careful" Nancy said. She turned to me. "So Ryan, how do you know Kara?" she asked. "I met her at her work and then started going to her dad's school" I said.

"I came along to help in any way that I can" I continued. "So, when are you planning to go to his club?" Nancy asked. "I am thinking in about a week" she said. "I'll give you a call later Nancy" Kara said as they both hugged each other. We both walked out the door. "Nice to have met you Ryan" Nancy said as she waved to both of us.

We spent the whole week training. Kara taught me some very advance techniques. "It is not necessary to hit your opponent" she said. "All you have to do is move around him" she said. It took me a while to believe this concept, it sounded crazy to me. "Isn't the point of fighting to hit the other person?" I asked. "In our system we use the opponent's body weight against him.

We use avoidance and we flow with their energy" she said. "You will get to a place where you won't think about what you are doing, you will just do it" she said. We worked on balance. Kara had two wide stumps in her backyard. She got me to stand on a stump and balance on one leg. "Get up and try again" she said every time I fell. Sometimes I would stand there for what seemed like hours. Every once in a while she got me to change legs. She stood on the other stump to support me.

She got me to spread my feet and bend my knees. "This is called a horse stance and it is really good for balance and for strengthening the legs" she said. "Along with physical training, I also had internal training, which consisted of changing my mindset from being negative, to being and speaking positive.

If you are hard on yourself and you speak negative words to yourself, it will affect your self-esteem and your self-confidence." she said. "You can defeat yourself before your opponent even touches you" she continued. "Your mind is very powerful, you can have all the moves, but if you think that you can't do something or win a fight, you won't even try" she said.

The phone rang at Nancy's home and she picked it up. "Hello Nancy" Kara said. "Hey Kara" she said. "You ready to go? We are going to come pick you up and strategize at my place" Kara said. "Okay, come on over" Nancy replied. We drove to get Nancy and brought her back. "Okay" Kara said as she put a black piece of paper on the table.

"The mafia boss's night club is here" she said as she drew a picture. The only way to get to it is through an alley" she continued. "He probably has bouncers outside the door" she said. "This will be the most dangerous thing we've done. If anyone wants out, step away right now" she said. We didn't move.

"Okay then" she said. "Let's go" she continued. We got in Kara's car and drove across the city. We parked the car a block away from the night club. We got out and started walking. We entered the alley and walked down it. We saw two bouncers in the distance and they saw us. "We walked up to them.

"We are here to see the mafia boss" I said to one of them. "Nobody sees the mafia boss" he said. "Tell him that we've got some business with him" I said. The bouncers stepped aside and let us in. We walked inside, music was blaring and waitresses were bringing drinks to people's tables. Smoke filled the air as people were dancing.

"Over there, in the back booth" Kara said as she pointed. "That's him" she said. "You sure?" I asked. "I'm positive" she said as we walked over to him. "Excuse me sir?" I asked as he turned. "Yes? What is it?" he asked. "Can we speak to you for a moment?"

I asked. "Of course, please sit" he said as he gestured for us to sit.

"What can I do for you?" he asked. "Well, your son killed my dad" Kara said. "Wait a second, I know you, you are Ledger's daughter" he said. "You have lots of guts coming here" he said. "Your father owed us lots of money, I had to make an example out of him. Since your father refused to pay us a percentage of the money he got, his debt now falls on you. You must pay, unless you can beat me at holding your breath under water.

"If you beat me, I will cancel the debt and you will be free to leave" he said. "Okay, I accept" she said. "Great let's go" he said as he led us to the back where there was a swimming pool. They both got in and submerged themselves as Nancy and I watched. A little while later, Kara began to rise to the surface, but she managed to wave her hands against the water and sunk down again.

The mafia boss sat on the bottom until he started to lose his breath. He rose to the top and jumped out of the water gasping for air. A few seconds later Kara jumped out of the water gasping for air. "You have to cancel my debt" she said as she looked at him. "Okay, consider it canceled, you can go" he said. We walked down the corridor of the night club and out the door.

"I changed my mind, I want the money" the mafia boss yelled. "No chance in hell" I yelled. He radioed to a sniper on top of the building. "When you see them, take them out" he said. We were walking down the alley to the car, when we heard a shot. We turned around and Nancy collapsed in Kara's arms.

Blood poured onto her arms as she set her down. "Run" I yelled as the sniper reloaded. As we ran down the alley, we got shot at a few more times, but he missed. We ran out of the alley and jumped in the car and drove to Kara's house. "Follow them, don't let them get away" the mafia boss said as he sent a hitman to kill us.

We went to the airport and got on a plane back to Sweden. The hitman saw us get on the plane and bought a ticket and got on the same plane. We stepped off the plane and drove to my house. "I need to talk to my family" I said. When we arrived at my house, we found the door wide open. We walked in, the place looked like it was robbed, everything was broken and stuff was on the floor.

I walked into the kitchen and saw everyone dead at the table. I dropped to my knees and wailed as Kara came into the kitchen. "Oh my god" she said as she covered her mouth. "I know exactly who did this, they are going to pay" I said as I grinded my teeth. Kara sat down beside me and hugged me. I held her tight and we both cried. "If only I would've been here, I could've done something" I said. "There was nothing you could have done" Kara said.

"We have to go, they will be back" Kara said. We walked out to her car and drove to her house. The next morning we were going to pick some stuff up at the store and found that Kara's tires were slashed. Uh oh, they found us, I thought. We started to run to the store and when we got there we looked around to see if we were followed.

Before we left the store, we looked out the windows to see if we could see anyone.

"Its all clear" I said as we walked outside. We walked all the way to Kara's house with no sign of anyone. "That's a good sign" I said as we unlocked the door and went inside. I turned on the news and the story of my family was all over the news. "*It was a brutal display of murder in this quiet town, this family was stabbed to death in their own kitchen and placed around the table in chairs. Possibly as a message to someone*" the news reporter said.

I turned off the television. "If he sent me a message, I'll send him one right back" I said. I decided to go back to my house to get their bodies so I could bury them. I got Kara to drive to my house and we loaded their bodies in her car. "Damn, that stinks" she said. "I know, but we have to give them a proper burial" I said. We brought them to the backyard and I dug graves to put them in.

Once I was done, we placed them in the graves and shoveled dirt on top of them. "I love you all so much, you were my best friends and I am going to miss you more than words can express. You were there for me in the good times as well as the bad times. We shared laughter and tears together, you will always be in my thoughts and in my heart" I said as I bowed my head. "For the brief time that I knew you guys, I knew that you guys were good people. You are never really gone, since you live on in Ryan" Kara said. "Thanks, that was beautiful" I said as I turned to her.

"It's important that I go back to *The Dark Panther* and get my father's body" she said. "I understand" I said as we got in her car and drove there. "Be on the lookout for Easter and his gang. We went inside and saw Ledger's body lying in the middle of the room. We were getting ready to pick his body up, when we saw Easter standing at the doorway. He threw a grenade at us. "Run" I screamed.

We both ran into Ledger's office as the grenade exploded, incinerating Ledger's body. A hitman was perched on the top of a building across the street and saw Easter. He took aim and shot him in the head as Easter dropped to the ground with a thud. His gang saw that he was dead and ran off. We went back in to where Ledger's body was. Once the smoke cleared, we looked but couldn't find his body anywhere.

We went outside and got in the car. She started the engine and the hitman shot out the back windshield. "Go go" I shouted as she sped off. We ran inside and sat at the table. "What are we going to do about that hitman?" she asked. "We have no choice, we must track him down and kill him, it is either him or us" I said as she nodded. "I want to say a few words about my father" she said.

"My father was a great man, he was humble and kind. He took good care of me, I loved him very much and now that he's gone, I feel lost. I am going to miss him like crazy" she said. "I didn't know him that well, but the time I did spend with him, I could tell he had a very gentle spirit and a compassionate heart" I said.

"I have an idea, let's lure him out into the country. That is where we will have the upper hand and can end this once and for all" I said. "Okay, let's do it" she said as she grabbed the keys to the car. She went upstairs to her dad's room, opened the closet and grabbed his gun. We started driving and sure enough a moment later, I saw a car following us in the distance.

"I know the perfect spot" Kara said as she turned onto a dirt road. The hitman had to slow down, because there was too much dust obstructing his view. We finally stopped an hour and a half down the road. We got out and ran into the trees. He drove up to our parked car and looked around to see if we were going to ambush him.

He got out and started looking around. We climbed up a hill and saw him walking on a path. "Give me the gun" I said as Kara handed me the sniper rifle. I set it up, aimed right at him and shot. He fell to the ground. "Finally this nightmare is over" I said as I looked at Kara.

Chapter 5
Re-opening *The Dark Panther*

"I think in memory of my dad, we should re-open *The Dark Panther*" Kara said. I took a sip of coffee. "Ya, that is a great idea" I replied. We had to re-build it, because the grenade that Easter threw at us destroyed everything. We got to work buying lumber. We nailed the floorboards in and put up the walls. We had to buy all new mats, because the old ones were destroyed. We bought new hand pads and kick pads.

We decided that we wanted to make the roof flat. We reinforced the roof with two by fours, so we could train on it. We nailed floorboards on it as well and we coated the boards with a sealer. We had to re-build the office. We made it double the size and put two desks in it for Kara and me.

We re-built the change rooms and put all new plumbing in. We worked day and night on the school until it was finished. We kept the name of the school the same in memory of Kara's dad.

We took an ad out in the paper introducing our re-opening. We waited and waited but nobody came. Then after a few days all of the old students started to come back and lots of new ones came to join. We explained to the old students that Ledger died and they all mourned for him. They all said great things about him.

"He was a great teacher" one student said. "He inspired me to keep up with my training" another student said. "His teachings will live on in us" another student said. "Thank you for your warm comments" Kara said. "It's good to have my old students back and a special welcome to all the new students. Would the new students please come to our office?" she asked. They all lined up in front of our office and one by one we interviewed them.

We asked each one why they wanted to learn Kung Fu. "I want to be able to hurt people" one student said. "Thank you for coming, but you are not what we are looking for" Kara said as she walked him out the front door. "I want to develop myself both mentally and physically" another student said.

"Great, just wait out in the lobby with all the other students please" I said. "I want to be able to learn how to defend myself if I need to" another student said. "Take a seat out in the lobby with the rest" Kara said. We got all the new student's measurements for their uniforms and we ordered them.

A lot of new students showed up, wanting to join, but we turned away half because of their reasons to learn. We walked into the lobby where all the students were. "Thank you all for coming and for your desire to learn. You all have been accepted into this school. And we are honored to have you here with us" I said. "All you new students may leave and come back tomorrow for your first day of training, all you old students stick around" Kara said.

"Just a reminder to everyone, that school fees will be three hundred dollars and will be due the first week of each month" I said. The new students turned and walked out the door. "We are so thrilled that you guys came back to train with us" I said. "It has been a rough couple of weeks. With the death of our teacher and the school getting destroyed" Kara said.

"You guys are in for a treat today, because we are going to learn something new. It is called the circle, it is very effective because instead of just standing in front of your opponent, you will be circling him." Kara said. "Ryan will show you" she said as I started to demonstrate. "Start with your left foot forward and you want to angle your toe so that it is facing the center, because that is where your opponent is going to be. Then you step with your right foot, you will naturally make a circle because your left foot is angled towards your opponent or center of the circle" I said.

"To go the other way, it is the same concept. But this time you toe in with the right foot, and step with your left foot" I continued. They began to try it, some of them got it, but most of them didn't. "That's okay, it is a new concept and we will work it until we get it" Kara said. We practiced the circle for an hour and a half.

"All right guys, you did great work today, I am very impressed with you all" I said. They all started to walk to the change rooms. "We are still going to have morning meditation classes, if anyone is interested in coming" Kara said as they all nodded.

After they left, Kara and I went to our office. We made a schedule of what days we were going to have the morning meditation. "We will tell the new students about morning meditation when they come in next" I said. We discussed who was going to teach what and when we were going to teach.

We stayed late figuring everything out. "We have to go home, I am exhausted" Kara said. "Ya okay, we can finish up tomorrow" I said as we locked the front door and drove home. We were so tired that we stumbled up the stairs, fell on our bed and went to sleep.

All the old students showed up for meditation the next morning. We all sat in the middle of the room and there was complete silence in the building. The meditation lasted for an hour. "Great class this morning guys" Kara said as we all opened our eyes.

"Wow, I feel super charged for the day" Jill said. "Ya, me too, I feel like I have so much energy" Paul said as the students walked to the change rooms. "Tonight we'll have the new students here, so do your best to make them feel welcome" Kara said as the students walked out the door.

Kara and I walked to school. When everyone saw me, their faces let me know that they were sorry for me. Word had spread all over the school that my family was murdered. They didn't know what to say to me, so they just hugged me and walked away. My teachers all expressed how sorry they were to hear about what happened.

"If you need more time off of school, I understand completely. I lost a family member and I was not myself for a few months" the principal said. "Thank you for your support, but I'll be fine" I said as I walked out of his office. "Before you go, I want to tell you that we're holding a memorial service for your brothers and sisters and Easter next week" he said.

When the bell rang for lunch, Kara and I were the only ones sitting at a table. I guess the other students were hesitant about what to say. "I'm afraid that everyone will treat me differently now" I said. "Ya, once you lose someone close to you, people don't know what to say to you anymore" Kara replied.

"So, are you going to the memorial service next week?" Kara asked. "I've already made my peace with their death, so going would just get me upset" I answered. "I understand" she said. "Are you going?" I asked. "No, I made my peace with them when you did" she said.

After school we went to *The Black Cup*, to see if we still had our jobs. "You can't just up and disappear for a week without telling me, I should fire you two, but I am willing to give you a second chance. Seeing that I'm short staffed, but don't do that again, because next time you will be gone" Roy said.

"Thank you" we both said as we went and got changed. We walked to our tills and started serving customers. Half way through our shift, a drunk man walked into the lobby. He started kicking signs and the other customers. One employee went over to him and asked him to leave. He turned around and punched her in the face.

I looked at Kara and went over to him. He tried to punch me, I grabbed his hand and put it behind his back. I then grabbed his other hand and put it behind his back also. Roy called the police and I kept him like that until they showed up.

"I want him out of here, he is being violent and disruptive. And he punched one of my employees in the face" Roy said. "Come on buddy, let's go" one of the officers said as both of them drug him out. He yelled and screamed as they put him in the back of their car. "Sorry about that folks" Roy said to the customers.

When we crossed the street to *The Dark Panther*, we saw a student waiting for us outside of the door. "You're early" I said to him. "Ya, I am so excited about my first day" he said. "Well come on in, Tom is it?' Kara asked. "Ya" he said as he followed us in. "You can just wait in the lobby until everyone gets here" I said.

"Okay" he said as he stood in the lobby. When everyone got there, we came out of the office with a pile of new uniforms. "Hello and welcome to all the new students, here are your uniforms" Kara said as she handed them to the new students. "You can all go get changed. Change rooms are around the corner, just follow the other students and then come back here" I said.

"First off, why don't we introduce ourselves to each other? We will start with ourselves and then go around the room" I said. "Kara and I are your instructors" I said. "My name is Chris" a tall, skinny boy said. "I'm John" a short, long hair boy said. "Sapphire" a tall girl said. "Pretty" a short girl with glasses said. "Lee" a chubby girl said. "Kristy" a girl with a nose ring said. "I'm Dan" a boy with a cut on his arm said.

"My name is Henry" a slim boy said. "Titanium" a boy with pimples on his face said. "Sam" a short boy said. "Matt" an older boy said. "Pat" a boy with a beard said. "Windy" a girl with purple hair said. "I'm Susie" a short girl with brown hair said. "Bridget" a young girl with braids said. "Chip" a rough looking boy said. "Josh" a muscular boy said. "Health" a boy with a scar on his hand said. "Jessica" a girl with a flower in her hair said.

"Kate" a girl with a big smile said. "April" a girl with blonde hair said. "I'm Jacob" a boy with green eyes said. "Joy" a girl with a butterfly tattoo on her wrist said. "Energy" a boy with a cast on his right leg said. "Melisa" a girl with black hair said. "Karl" a boy with glasses said. "Set" a boy with spiked hair said. "I'm Simmer" a girl with long red hair said. "Jeff" a boy with really white teeth. "And I'm Charly" a frightened looking girl said.

"Once again, I am glad that all of you are here" I said. "We just have a couple rules, we want each of you to get either a full time or part time job. We don't want you telling people how good you are at fighting, because they will challenge you. And lastly, we don't want you starting fights. If we find out that any of you break these rules, you will be kicked out of this school, understood?" Kara asked.

All the students nodded. "Understood" they all yelled. "Great, let's begin" I said. "Let's split up, I want all the advance students to go over to the mat and all the new students will stay here" Kara said. Kara led the advance students to the mat, while I stayed with the new students.

"Okay, first let's work on what are called cover hands. One hand protects the upper part of your body and one hand protects the lower part of your body. So, if your opponent throws a punch, you can block it with your upper hand. And if he throws a kick, you can protect the lower part of your body." I said.

It is very important that you keep your hands in this position at all times and make sure you tuck your elbows in as tight as you can to your body, like this" I said as I showed them. "Now you try it" I said as I watched them do it.

Kara worked with the advanced students on some trapping and throwing techniques. She looked at the clock after a while. "Wow, where did the time go?" she asked. "Okay guys, that's it for today, great work" she said as they joined the beginner students. "There will be no morning meditation class tomorrow, we will resume in the evening" I said.

"You are dismissed" Kara said as they all walked to the change rooms. "Awesome class today" John said as he walked out. Kara and I went to our office, sat down and calculated everyone's school fees. We wrote them out on a chart and put it behind our desks so that we could see. "Make sure you add in the cost of their uniforms for the first month" Kara said.

"I will" I said as I put a memo on the chart. It was another late night, we stayed there until we almost fell asleep. We got up and stumbled to the car. On the way home I could barely keep my eyes open. We stumbled up the stairs, hit the bed and were out cold. We slept like babies all through the night.

We went in to *The Dark Panther* in the morning, even though we didn't have class. We tidied up the lobby and put the hand and kick pads away. We went in the change rooms and made sure they were all clean. Then we locked the front door and walked to school.

Somehow word started getting around at school that we had a Kung Fu school. Students kept coming up to us. "Can I join?" they would ask. A lot of students asked. We could tell which ones were serious about it and which ones weren't. The ones that were serious, we told to drop by and we would interview them. We gave them the name of our school and the address. Even some of the teachers came up to ask us if they could join. We turned some of them down, but some were really interested, so we told them to drop by as well.

We walked into math class and sat down. It was weird, almost half the class wasn't there. The teacher came in a minute later. "Despite what you might have heard about the weather today, this is not a skip and go to the beach day. I applaud all of you for not giving in to peer pressure and taking the day off" the teacher said.

"The ones that are not here, are going to miss this little test and will take a zero on it" he continued as he handed out the test. "Just do your best, I didn't expect you to study for this, so don't worry" he said. It took us all class to write the test. When the bell rang, we brought them up to his desk on our way out.

Work flew by so fast, there was a constant line up of customers. We walked out the door and hurried to *The Dark Panther*. We were eager to see who from school would show up. Nobody from our school showed up, only our current students. "Maybe they need time to think about it" Kara said. "Ya, maybe" I replied.

The students poured into the lobby from the change rooms. "Okay" I said as I rubbed my hands together. "Today we are going to keep both groups together. It might get a bit crowded in here, so spread out" Kara said. "We are going to work on smoothness and flowing of your movements" I said.

"Don't worry new students, we are not going to do anything too difficult" I said. "Close your eyes, I want you all to imagine that you are in water. I want you to take your hands and move them through the water. Take your left hand and flow it up with your palm to the ceiling.

Now flow it down with your palm to the ground. Then take your right hand, flow it up with your palm to the ceiling and flow it down with your palm to the ground. There should be no jerky movements and no stopping. Your hands should flow up and flow down" Kara instructed.

She demonstrated as she talked. "Now, you guys try it" she said as her and I walked around. "Good, a little jerky in your movements, smooth it out" I said to John. "To avoid the jerky movements, you must get rid of all the tension in your arms" I said. "It takes time to achieve it, but it will definitely come" Kara said. "Meditation is a great tool to help release tension, not just in your arms, but all over your body" she continued.

They all stood there doing the movements for half an hour. "Okay, let's move on, but I want you to practice that at home" I said. "For you new students, there are two basic stances. A right fighting stance and a left fighting stance. In the left fighting stance, you slide your right foot over and back just a bit and angle both toes to the right.

The right is the opposite, you drop the left foot to the side and angle both toes to the left" she said. "Now I want to move into some basic kicks from a left fighting stance" Kara said as she demonstrated. "This is called a toe snap kick, you raise your knee up to your hip level, you snap out the foot and you make contact with the top of the foot" she said. "Once again, here is what it looks like" she said as she made sure everyone could see. "Now you try it" she said. "I want ten from the left stance and ten from the right stance" she said.

"One…two…three…four…five…six…seven…eight…nine…and ten…" she counted. "Now the right side, one…two…three…four…five…six…seven…eight…nine…and ten…, good job" she said. "Close your eyes, bend your knees and just relax in this position. Now I want you to see yourself going into a perfect right stance. Your toes are turned to the left, you are bringing that knee up to your hip level, snapping your foot and hitting with the top" I said.

"Open your eyes, get into your right stance and do a toe snap kick" Kara said. After the students did it, they were shocked. "Oh wow, that is amazing" Josh said. "That is a great tool" Melisa said. "It is a great tool, because whatever the mind thinks of, the body does" I said. "That concludes this class guys, see you tomorrow. We are going to have meditation in the morning for those who are able to make it, if you can't, try to find a quiet place and meditate by yourself" Kara said as everyone headed to the change rooms.

Kara and I left early. We got home before it got dark outside and cooked some supper. After supper, we went out to the backyard and did some training. "I am going to show you some sweeping techniques. This is when you take your leg and you sweep it under your opponent's leg to knock him over" she said. "Never sweep with your back leg, always sweep with your front leg. Because if you use your back leg you can fall off balance" she said.

"Get into your right stance and I will get into my left stance. Now with your right foot, I want you to sweep my left foot. When you do, don't lean back, lean into me" she said as I tried it. "Good, good" she said. "Now get into your left stance and I will get in my right. Take your left foot and sweep my right foot" she said as I tried it and knocked her down. "Great" she said as she got to her feet. We practiced that same technique for an hour.

"Now let's move onto how to get out of headlocks" she said as she told me to put her in a headlock. "What you do is, you drop your chin to your chest, turn your head to the side. Put your hand on their elbow and flip their hand away. Then they end up with their back towards you and you can do all kinds of things at this point" she instructed.

We went for a walk and talked about Kung Fu. She told me things that I didn't know about and she mentioned again how important internal training is. "Internal training is what separates us from the others. Internal training makes us look inside of ourselves. We start to develop discipline, honor, respect, integrity and humility" she said.

"We don't have to prove anything to anyone, just to ourselves. You will start to view yourself differently, you will view other people differently and you will view the world differently" she said. "It's really quite amazing, you learn to control yourself.

You learn to control your emotions and you learn to control what you think. When negative thoughts come your way, you just shrug them off. You will get mentally strong, as well as physically strong. You will be disciplined to say no to things that you used to say yes to" she said.

"You develop a deeper appreciation for life and for people. Your senses increase as you practice listening and observing. You start to pick up on things that other people never would have" she said. "Some people learn this art and use it for evil. That is why it is very important you understand who your student is and what he is capable of. I never train anyone with anger problems, because you never know if he will use this art the next time he has an outburst" she continued.

We walked around the corner and came to a pie shop. We went in and ordered two blueberry pies. We sat down outside on the balcony, which overlooked a river. "Mmm this is so good" I said as I looked at Kara. "Ya, it is" she replied. We finished the pie, headed down to the river and walked beside it.

"I like to train right beside the river, the sound of it is calming" she said. In the distance we saw a man running and a moment later we saw a cop running. "Don't you want to go and stop that man?" I asked. "No, that's the cop's job, besides, it is a bad idea to get involved in other people's messes" she answered.

Chapter 6
Strange Things Are Happening

When we got back to the house, we saw on the front door the words *you're next*. "Who the hell did this?" I asked. "Must have just been some kids" Kara said as she went in the house and got some cleaning supplies. It took her half an hour to get those words off the door. "There, all done" she said as she walked into the kitchen and sat down beside me.

"Let's go to bed, we have to get up to lead the meditation class" I said as we walked upstairs. We woke up in the middle of the night to the sound of a window being broken. "I'll check it out, you go back to sleep" I said as I walked downstairs. I saw a brick in the middle of the family room and a big hole in the window.

"Oh crap, who would do something like this?" I asked myself. I got a piece of cardboard and taped up the hole for the night. I went back upstairs. "What was it?" Kara asked. "Someone threw a brick through the window" I answered. "I will deal with it tomorrow, let's go back to sleep" I said as I kissed her.

We got up really early and drove to *The Dark Panther*. We did our own meditation before the students came. We sat in silence for forty five minutes. When we opened our eyes, we both had a look of total relaxation on our faces. Our students started to come in and walked up to us. "Go get changed and meet us back here" Kara said. They came out and sat on the floor.

"Today we are going to do something different. After the meditation, we are going to say positive things to ourselves out loud" she said. Kara and I could see as the students were meditating that it was changing their demeanor. They were smiling and they looked relaxed. Half an hour passed by. "Okay, everyone open your eyes, now tell me how you feel?" I asked.

"I feel calm" Sapphire said. "I feel lighter" Windy said. "I feel like I am present in this moment" Karl said. "I feel energized"

Jeff said. "Awesome, it's a great feeling isn't it?" Kara asked as they all nodded. "Okay, now we are going to speak positive things about ourselves, Kara will start" I said.

"I am beautiful" Kara said. "I am smart" I said. "I am strong" Chris said. "I am loved" John said. "I trust myself" Sapphire said. "I believe in myself" Pretty said. "I am proud of myself" Lee said. "I am true to myself" Kristy said. "I know who I am" Dan said. "I am worth it" Henry said. "I deserve to be happy" Titanium said. "I go after what I want" Sam said.

"Goodness follows me" Matt said. "I take care of myself" Pat said. "I appreciate myself" Windy said. "I have lots of self-esteem" Susie said. "I have a positive self-image" Bridget said. "I am wonderful" Chip said. "I take action" Josh said. "I have discipline" Health said. "Good things happen to me" Jessica said.

"Love surrounds me" Kate said. "I am brave" April said. "I am healthy" Jacob said. "I make wise decisions" Joy said. "I receive love" Energy said. "I give out love" Melisa said. "Today will be a good day" Karl said. "I am courageous" Set said. "I am confident" Simmer said. "I love to smile" Jeff said. "Beauty is all around me" Charly said.

"What do you notice about the atmosphere in this room?" Kara asked. "There is love in here" Simmer said. "Right, there is so much positive energy, you can change the dynamics of the room by speaking positive words" she continued. "Remember that next time you are in a room with a negative energy to it. Just speak some positivity into the air and it will knock out the negativity" I said.

"Thank you all for coming, we will see you this evening. Have a great day and remember, think positive and you'll be positive" Kara said. Kara and I stayed sitting while everyone else got up and went to the change rooms. When they left, we closed our eyes and continued to meditate. "We better go to school" Kara said as she opened her eyes and looked at her watch.

"All students and teachers to the theater right now" the principal said over the intercom. We entered the theater class by class and sat down in our seats. I leaned over to Kara. "This is the play that Mike, Dream, Jay, and Dish were supposed to be in" I whispered to her. Half way into the play, I started to cry thinking about them. I leaned over to Kara.

"I have to get out of here" I whispered as I got up and walked out of the theater. Kara came out after me. "I was just thinking about how I watched them practice in front of me and now they are gone" I said as I sobbed. Kara put her arm around me and hugged me.

"I know you miss them, I miss them too" she said as she started to cry. "I can't go back in there" I said. "I understand" she said as we walked to the student lounge. We waited there until the bell rang for lunch. We were the first ones in there, so we got our pick of whatever table we wanted.

Again when we got to *The Dark Panther,* we didn't see any of the students or teachers from school. The students began to pile in the door and went to the change rooms. They came back, talking very loudly. "Okay, quiet down please" I said as they all stood there in silence.

"You may notice as you look around that some of the students are gone" Kara said. "That is because they broke the rules and dishonored everything that this club stands for and we will not tolerate that" I said. "What did they do?" Joy asked. "They were starting fights on purpose with people" Kara said.

"This is completely unacceptable. We were sad to let them go, but we can't have that kind of behavior in this school" I said. "Okay, let's split into three groups and start circle walking with the right side in on the circle" Kara said as the students separated. "This is what an inside change looks like" I said as I showed them. "You toe in slightly with your left foot, then you pick up your right foot and take a step, so that you are going the other way" I continued.

"Let's try that" Kara said as both her and I led everyone in walking. "Now let's do it from the left side in. Toe in slightly with your right foot and step with your left foot, so you end up going in the opposite direction" she said. We did that for half an hour. "Okay, everyone come back to the middle" I said.

"Let's do what's called a heel thrust kick. It is just like the toe snap, but one difference. When you bring your knee up to your hip, you thrust out your heel" Kara said. We practiced it for a while. "Why aren't we learning anything cool, like how to flip people?" Set asked.

"That is way down the road of your training, first you must learn the basics. Without a solid foundation in the basics, you will never become any good" I said. He was silent after that. "How long will it take to get really good?" Sam asked. "A while, you have to trust the process, we will tell you" Kara said.

The next day flew by, school and work were a blur. Before we knew it, it was time for class. "Has anyone seen Set?" Kara asked as she looked around. "No, I don't know where he is" Pretty said. "He might be sick" Susie said. "Everyone sit facing the front, I want everyone to watch two people go over to the sparring mats and do some slow speed sparring" I said.

Dan and Joy got up in front of everyone. "Okay, you can begin" I said as they started. "Slow it down, you're going too fast" Kara said. "More relaxation in your arms" I said. "Okay, you two can sit down" I said after a minute. "And you two can go up" Kara said as she pointed to Windy and Matt. Matt started throwing punches and Windy got scared and ran.

"It's alright to be scared Windy, but you must learn to face your fears" I said as she went back over and resumed sparring. Kara turned to the students. "We must control our reactions and not let them control us" she said.

"Very good, sit down guys" Kara said. "We will get April and Kate up front" I said as they walked in front of the class. "Get your hands up Kate and keep them up, don't drop them" Kara said. "Once you drop your cover hands, you will get taken apart by your opponent. He will see his opportunity and take it" I said as I turned around to the students.

"Okay, thank you to those who came up and sparred in front of the class. I know that it might have been a bit nerve racking to spar in front of the whole class, but you did it" Kara said. "Next class we will get more students up there" I said. "Let's all stand up and take a deep breath. And now release it and take another one and release it" Kara said.

"We will see you all for morning meditation tomorrow" I said as everyone went to the change rooms. When the last student left, we locked the door and went to our office. "I thought tonight went pretty well didn't you?" I asked. "Ya, it was a good introduction for them" Kara said. We spent the next three hours planning out what we were going to teach tomorrow. When we got home, we sat out on our balcony with a cup of tea.

"I have an idea, why don't we get the students to write down one thing that they would like to learn" I said. "That is a great idea, I mean if the students want to do something really advance we won't do it, but within reason" Kara said.

"What do you think happened to Set? Do you think he was sick? Or do you think he dropped out?" Kara asked. "Honestly, I think he dropped out" I said. "Should we tell the other students" Kara asked. "I think so, they have a right to know" I said.

As we were walking in the house, something hit me in the back. I turned and looked around, but I didn't see anyone. "Did you see that?" I asked. "What?" Kara asked. "Someone just hit me in the head" I said. "Really?" she asked. "Ya, you didn't see that?" I asked. "No" she replied as we continued to walk in the house. We drove to the glass shop to replace the window that was broken last night. We brought it home and I installed it.

"There, good as new" I said as we went upstairs. A loud crash made us both spring up in bed in the middle of the night. "What the hell was that?" Kara asked. "I don't know, but it was loud" I said. "Go check it out" Kara said. "Okay" I said as I flung the covers off me and went downstairs. I saw another brick in the middle of the floor. I looked at the window and it was smashed.

"Damn it" I whispered under my breath. "You are never going to believe this"

I said as I walked into our room. "What?" she asked. "The window is broken again and there is another brick on the floor" I said. "Really?" she asked. "Let me see" she said as she got out of bed and followed me downstairs. "Who the hell would do this?" she asked. "I don't know, but this is no coincidence" I said.

We drove to *The Dark Panther* early the next morning, sat down and started meditating. We sat there in silence for fifteen minutes and then the students started showing up. They saw that we were meditating and quietly got changed in the change rooms and sat down with us. We didn't say a word as they sat around us, but we knew they were there.

A few of the students were fidgeting around, they were having trouble concentrating. They finally found their center and were quiet for the rest of the session. The only sound was the occasional deep breath that was taken every once in a while. Half an hour passed by and Kara and I opened our eyes.

"How is everyone feeling?" she asked. "Good, ready to take on the day" Energy answered. "What I want to do now is, whoever wants to, can randomly blurt out things that they are thankful for or things that they love and that make them happy" Kara said. "I am thankful for my life" Jessica said.

"I love my hair" April said. "I am thankful for my family" Jeff said. "Sunshine makes me happy" Kate said. "Hearing the birds chirp makes me happy" Matt said. "I am thankful for my health" Susie said. "Awesome, good job guys, we'll see you tonight, have a great day" I said as Kara and me stood up.

"No sleeping in class" the teacher said to Kara. "Sorry, I didn't have a very good sleep last night" she said. "Make sure you get a better sleep tonight" the teacher said. "I plan to" she replied. We both were so tired, we went to the student lounge at lunch and slept until the bell woke us up.

"I'll see you after school" Kara said as she kissed me and we walked to our classes. When the bell rang at the end of the day,

Kara was waiting for me out front. We talked all the way to *The Black Cup*. Our shift didn't start for another half an hour, so we got a coffee, sat at a booth and talked. We changed and started our shift. It was a great shift, all the customers were very nice and respectful.

When our students arrived at *The Dark Panther*, we waited for them to get changed and seated. "We got confirmation that Set in fact quit, there are no hard feelings, that is just the way it is. Not everyone is cut out for Kung Fu, not everyone is disciplined enough and not everyone is willing to make the sacrifices required to train and advance" Kara said.

"Now, what we want to ask of you is, what is one thing that you would like to learn? And we will teach it, in reason. It can't be something that a master does. I am going to pass pieces of paper around and a hat. Write down what you want to learn and put it in the hat. Then Ryan and I will go through them tonight after class" Kara said. I handed out the paper and the hat. Kara and I waited a few minutes while they thought about what to put in the hat.

"There will be no morning meditation tomorrow" I said. "I will soon put up a schedule of when the meditation sessions will be held" I continued. The class went by very fast. When all the students left, we went through the hat in our office. When we finished going through them, we found that most of them were doable. Only some of the requests were too advanced for the students. "Maybe in a few years" I said to Kara as I looked at the advanced requests.

On our way home we had to stop off at the glass shop to pick up another pane of glass. We got home, and I put it in. "Nobody better break it this time" I said threateningly. We sat outside with a cup of tea. "It's such a nice night, look at all the stars" Kara said. "Ya, they're beautiful" I responded. "It's late, we should get some sleep" I said as I led her inside.

We walked up stairs and went to sleep. We slept through the whole night. I sprang out of bed in the morning and ran downstairs. "Yes, no brick" I yelled.

"Awesome" she replied. I went into the kitchen and made some coffee for us. I took it up to her and we lay there in bed sipping our coffee and talking.

That night when we came home, we were pleased to find that the window wasn't smashed. "I don't know who smashed it those two times, but we don't have to worry about that anymore" I said. We took our tea and went out on the back balcony. We got up and started to spar with each other. "Wow, you are improving very fast Ryan" Kara said.

"Thanks, you're a good teacher" I said. Every time I tried to sweep her leg she pulled it back. "I can't get your leg" I said. "I know, I don't want you to" she replied. After a while we stopped, sat back down and finished off our tea while watching the stars. We woke up the next morning and as we left the house, we glanced over at the window and saw that it was still intact.

We got to school really early. We sat on the front lawn and meditated until the other students started to show up. "Sorry I never came by *The Dark Panther*, but I was thinking about whether I wanted to join, I'll come by tonight" two of the teachers and some of the students said to me at lunch. "Looks like we could have some new students" I said as Kara smiled.

When we left at the end of the day, it started to rain, so we ran to *The Black Cup*. "What's wrong Roy?" I asked when I saw that he was upset. "The others called in sick and I am short staffed. Do you think you two can stay later tonight?" he asked. "Sure, I just have to go to *The Dark Panther* in a bit and tell my students that there will be no class tonight.

"Ya, no problem" he said. "Thank you guys so much, any cakes that you want are free tonight for you" he continued. He wasn't kidding, it was only him, Kara and me working. Incredibly, we made it work. We stayed all the way up until it closed. We watched as the last customer left and then we changed and left.

"Let's do some training when we get home, because we missed out tonight" Kara said. "Ya, okay, I am up for that" I said. After we finished, we went up to bed. I got up in the middle of the night and heard a loud smash. I ran downstairs to see a brick on the floor again. I looked out the window and saw a figure start to run. I dashed out the door chasing him.

Chapter 7
This Has Got To Stop

I ran down the street after him. I turned the corner and lost him in a sea of people. "Damn" I yelled as I searched for him. I went up to a few people, thinking they were him. When I turned them around, they were someone else. I gave up hope and turned around and began to walk home. When out of the corner of my eyes I saw him look at me and start to run.

I started to chase after him. He ran as fast as he could and I followed right behind him. He ran up to the entrance of the train station, where there was a lineup of people. He shoved people out of the way to get through. He ran on to a train right before it was about to leave. "Get out of the way" I yelled as I pushed through the lineup of people. I stopped running when I got to the train platform, just as it was taking off.

I was going to catch him at the next stop, so I ran to the next platform. I saw the next train pull in, I checked all the people who got off, but nobody fit the description of who I was looking for. I got on the train and searched, but he wasn't there. "That's weird" I said as I started to walk back home.

"Did you get him?" Kara asked. "No, I don't know what happened to him" I said as I went into the kitchen to make some coffee. "I was so sure that I would get him" I said as I poured a cup for Kara and for me. We sat out on the balcony, since there was no meditation class scheduled. "It's a beautiful morning, the birds are chirping, the sun is shining and there is not a cloud to be seem" Kara said as she took a sip of her coffee.

"So our graduation is coming up in two months and then no more school. We can then concentrate fully on *The Dark Panther*" I said. "Ya, it'll be nice not to do homework" Kara said. We sat out on the balcony for another ten minutes and finished our coffee. We got in the car and left for school. When we got there, there were no parking spots, so we had to park one block away and walk.

We went for a walk at lunch. We walked a ways away from the school. In the distance I saw someone that looked very familiar. I didn't recognize him right away.

Then it hit me, that was the guy who I was chasing, I got him now, I thought. "That is the guy Kara" I said. We both started chasing him as he saw us running towards him in the distance. He ran to his car, got in and drove off. "Not again" I yelled. We hurried back to school before the bell rang.

When we got to *The Black Cup*, I told Roy that I couldn't work. I had to interview potential students for the school. "Do you both need it off?" Roy asked. "No, just me, Kara can stay" I said. "Okay, you can have tonight off" Roy said. "Thank you Roy" I said as I walked out the door and walked to *The Dark Panther*. I went to my office and waited for the new students to show up.

I wasn't at all surprised, only half of them showed up. Two teachers showed up and five students from school. I greeted them and walked them into the lobby. "Okay, I'll bring you one by one into my office and interview you" I said as I brought the first student into my office. "Have a seat" I said as I pointed to a chair.

I shook his hand. "My name is Ryan" I said. "I'm Logan" he said. "Nice to meet you

Logan" I said. "Tell me why you want to learn Kung Fu" I said as I leaned back in my chair. "Well, I've always been interested in it, my grandfather used to do it and would tell me stories about his training" Logan said.

"And do you think it is something that you will stick with or is it just an activity that you'll eventually get tired of?" I asked. "This is something that I would like to do for my whole life" he said. "Okay, thank you Logan, you can wait with the others, please send the next student in" I said.

"Have a seat please" I said. "My name is Ryan" I said. "And what is your name?" I asked. "Ashley" she said. "And why do you want to learn Kung Fu?" I asked. "I have a friend who practices it and she says that it develops you mentally as well as physically" she answered. "Interesting" I said as I wrote what she said down on a piece of paper.

"Okay, thank you, you can wait outside with the others, can you send the next one in?" I asked. As she walked out to the lobby, she looked at the closest one to the door. "You can go in now" she said. He walked in the room. "Sit down please" I said as he sat.

"How are you? My name is Ryan" I said. "My name is Cheer" he said. "Why do you want to learn Kung Fu?" I asked. "I need to learn how to protect myself" he said. "Okay, thank you, have a seat with the others in the lobby, send the next one in" I said.

"My name is Ryan, what is your name?" I asked as the next student came in and sat down. "My name is Dragon" he said. "Why do you want to learn Kung Fu?" I asked. "I want to defend my honor" he said. "What do you mean, your honor?" I asked. "I need to keep my reputation of being a hard ass" he said. "Okay, thank you" I said. "Next" I yelled. "Have a seat" I said as the next student came in and sat down.

"What is your name?" I asked. "My name is Fay" she said. "Nice to meet you, my name is Ryan" I said. "Why do you want to learn Kung Fu?" I asked. "I need to be able to defend myself" she said. "Why?" I asked. "Some of the boys get a little too aggressive when I turn them down" she said. "Thank you, you can send in the other student now" I said.

"Hello, how are you?" I asked as I shook the next student's hand. "I am good, thanks" he replied. "What's your name?" I asked. "My name is Rob" he said. "Why do you want to learn Kung Fu?" I asked. "I am looking for a hobby that is fun and challenging" he said. "Well, Kung Fu is definitely challenging" I said. "Thank you, can you send in the last student please?" I asked.

The last student came into my office and sat down. "What is your name?" I asked. "Milo" he said. "Nice to meet you, I'm Ryan" I said as I shook his hand. "Why do you want to learn Kung Fu?" I asked. "I want to understand myself better" he said. "Really? Explain" I asked. "Well, I want to get in touch with myself, others and the world around me" he said. "I have to tell you that is the best explanation I have ever heard and what I love to hear" I said. "Join the others in the lobby" I said.

I walked into the lobby where all the students were sitting. "Thank you all so much for taking time out of your day to come down here. I'll see you all here tomorrow night and I will explain more about the rules" I said as I walked them out the door. I locked up *The Dark Panther* and went to wait for Kara to get off work.

I walked in just as she was finishing with a customer. She looked at me and smiled. "Have a seat, I'll bring you a coffee, I'm almost done, just a few more minutes" she said as I sat at the booth beside the window. She came over to me, handed me a coffee and sat down across from me "So, how did the interviews go?" she asked. "Most of them went very well" I said.

"Most of them?" she asked. "Ya, some of them weren't serious, I don't want to have them as our students" I said. Roy came out just before we left. "Thanks again Roy" I said. "You're welcome" he said as the door swung shut behind me.

The next day after school, we couldn't wait until work was over so we could get to *The Black Panther.* One by one the students started to show up. They went immediately to the change rooms and then came to the lobby. "Hi everyone, I hope you had a great day, we reviewed what you wrote down on the pieces of paper the other day. Some of the requests we are not going to learn because they are too advance for you guys at this stage in the game" Kara said.

She picked up the hat and randomly picked one out. "Okay, tonight we are going to learn back angle kicks" she said as she read the piece of paper. "Let's start with a warm up, to get the blood flowing" I said as I started to jump up and down. They followed and then I started to jump forward and backwards, which they also followed.

"Now that we got the blood flowing, we will begin. Get into your right fighting stance, from here you are going to look over your left shoulder. Lift your left knee up to about hip level and thrust your leg backwards" I said as I demonstrated. "I'll show you again" I said as I demonstrated again. "Okay, now you guys try it" Kara said. "Now I will show you from the left fighting stance, it is pretty much the same.

The only thing that's different is that you use your right leg to kick" I said as I showed them. "You guys give it a try" Kara said as we both watched them do it a couple times. "Good job, you can also do it from the circle. What you do is, before you kick, you have to turn your feet so that your heels are pointed to the center or your opponent.

Remember, wherever your heels are pointed, that is where your kick is going to end up. So always have your heels facing your opponent" Kara said as she showed them. "You guys try it" I said as we watched. "What happens if you hit your opponent with the side of your foot?" Windy asked. "Good question, does anybody know?" I asked, but nobody said anything.

"You bring it back right away and keep trying. It is very important that you never get fixated on the fact that you didn't get the technique right. We all make mistakes and practice makes perfect. If you work it enough, it will become like breathing for you" I said. "Another point I'll mention is, if you don't land the technique don't be upset, don't sit there and cry about it. Keep moving, and keep throwing techniques. If you focus on the one that you didn't land, you take your focus off of your opponent" Kara said.

An hour and a half went by before I looked at my watch. "Okay guys, that was good work tonight, I want you all to practice those back angle kicks" I said. "Morning meditation is on for tomorrow, if you didn't check the schedule. We will see you then, have a great night, don't get discouraged, you are progressing, even if it feels like you're not" Kara said.

As everyone started to leave, Kara and I went to our office to work. We had to add the new students to the lists. "We better go, we still have to stop off at the hardware store to pick up that pane of glass" I said as we packed up. We pulled up in front of the house and saw a bunch of people standing around our window. "Get out of here" I yelled as they all ran.

We looked inside to see what everyone else was looking at. There was another brick on our living room floor. It was glowing and was shooting beams of light in every direction. "What the hell?" Kara asked. The beams of light disappeared and a countdown began. I turned to Kara. "Run for it" I yelled as I grabbed her hand and we dashed down the street. We heard a loud explosion, looked back and saw our home burning in flames.

"There goes our beautiful home" Kara said. I looked over towards the park and saw that same guy again. He was watching our home burn with a smile on his face. "Look over there, this time I got him" I said as I ran towards him. He saw me and started running as I chased him down the street. He turned the corner and got hit by a truck.

I turned the corner to see him lying there, face down in the middle of the street. I ran up to him and turned him over. He wasn't a man at all, he was a woman. What was going on? I thought, now I can't ask her why she did this. I searched her pockets. I found a card with my mom's name on it and another card with the mafia boss's name on it.

I walked back to where Kara was. "Well, did you get him?" she asked. "He turned out to be a she and by the time I caught up with her, I found her dead in the street" I said. "I found two cards in her pocket, one with my mom's name on it and one with the mafia boss's name on it" I said.

"I was hoping this was over, but it looks like we are still in the middle of it" Kara said. "We will have to go to China again to finish this, but for tonight we will have to stay at a hotel" she continued. "Why would she have a card with my mom's name on it?" I asked as we walked to a hotel. "They were probably following her. The mafia boss is ruthless and he won't stop until he is satisfied" I said.

"I am sorry that I got you involved in all of this, it is my fault that this happened" Kara said as she dropped her head. "I need some time by myself to think and to process all of this" I said. "I understand" she replied. I walked out of our hotel room. "Wait Ryan, I'm sorry" she said as I disappeared around the corner. I walked for hours, trying to make sense of all of this.

I walked up and down the streets. I was still very upset over my family's murder. I needed to come up with a plan to stop the mafia boss, before Kara and I wind up dead. I walked back to the hotel room that we were staying in. "Ryan, thank god you're back, how are you feeling?" Kara asked. "A little better,

I've been thinking about what we have to do about this. We have to end this or he will keep sending hitman after hitman to try and finish the job" I said.

"I tried to think of a way that we can settle this without violence, but I can't see a way" I continued. "You're right, we have to kill him, it is the only way this will stop" Kara said. "I also thought about what to tell our students, we'll have to close *The Dark Panther* for a few weeks. And we also have to see if we can take some time off work" I said.

"We can tell them tomorrow during morning meditation" Kara said. "Good thing last day of classes are tomorrow" I said. "If we had to miss school, we wouldn't have graduated" Kara said. Just then we heard a knock at the door and Kara went to answer it. "Hello" Kara said. "Hello, my name is Albert and I was wondering if I could use your phone. My car broke down and I need to call a tow truck" he said.

"Why don't you use the phone in the lobby?" she asked. "Because I don't have any change with me" he said. "All right, fine" she said as she opened the door and let him in. "Thank you" he said as he walked over to the phone. He dialed, then a moment later he pulled out a knife.

He ran at Kara, she stepped out of the way, took his knife and whipped Albert around, sending him crashing to the floor. He got up and lunged at her with his knife. She stepped out of the way, kicked his knife out of his hand and kicked him in the chest. He flew backwards ten feet, making a dent in the wall and crumbled to the ground.

I came around the corner, fresh from my shower. "What happened here?" I asked. "I'm guessing another hitman from the mafia boss" Kara said. "Check his pockets" I said as Kara hunted through his pockets. "Look at this" she said. I walked over and saw directions to *The Dark Panther*. "How did he know where our school was?" I asked.

"I don't know, but we have to shut it down right away" Kara said. "What's this?" I asked as I saw a red light flashing from his back pocket. I took it out. "Look what we have here" I said as I pulled out a radio. "I wonder who he was talking to" Kara said.

"*Come in alpha leader*" the mafia boss said on the radio. "I knew it" I said. "We must leave for China tomorrow" I continued.

Our hotel was only a block away from *The Dark Panther,* so we walked. We got there early so we could do some meditation before the others came. Ten minutes later, noise filled the air as the students started to walk in. "Go and get changed" Kara said as she opened her eyes. They all came back a few moments later, sat on the floor, closed their eyes and sat in silence.

"If you're having trouble sitting still this morning, focus on your breathing. Breathe in deeply and then breathe out. Breathe in deeply and then breathe out. This will bring your focus back to the present moment in time" I said. "Okay, great class today, there won't be any class for the next month.

Ryan and I will be going out of the country to handle some personal issues. We apologize for the short notice, but this issue just popped up" Kara said. "Just continue to practice by yourself and with the other students. And before you know it, we will be back" I said.

As we were walking up the stairs to the front door of the school, students were hollering and yelling. "Ya, last day of school" they shouted. We went inside and saw balloons and streamers everywhere. We said goodbye to all of our teachers. We hugged and wished our friends the best. Everyone was going around getting others to sign their yearbook and getting their yearbook signed.

"*To all the grade twelve students, I wish you all the best in your future. To those of you that we'll see next year, enjoy your summer*" the principal said on the school intercom. "*There is cake in the lobby for everyone*" he continued. When the bell rang at the end of the day, all the student screamed for joy.

Everyone was rushing to get out of the school as fast as possible to start their summer vacation. As we were walking, out of the corner of my eye I saw a car driving slowly beside us. They rolled down the back window a little and stuck the barrel of a gun out and unloaded at us. "Run" Kara screamed as we both dived into some shrubs and crawled on our bellies to safety. "Holy crap, that was close" I said.

We went back through the shrubs and saw two students dead on the sidewalk. We didn't know what to do, so we just kept walking. We got to *The Black Cup* and went in to find Roy. We walked to the back and found him in his office. "Why don't you talk to him while I change?" Kara asked as she went to the change room. "Hi Roy, can I talk to you for a second?" I asked. "Sure you can" he said as he shut his door.

"Kara and I just found out about some personal issues and we have to go out of the country for a month. Is it okay if we have that time off?" I asked. "That's a long time, ya, you can have the time off. And when you come back, your jobs will be waiting for you" Roy said. "Thanks Roy, you're so generous" I said. "When do you leave?" he asked. "Maybe tonight, if we can, if not, then tomorrow" I said.

It was very quiet at *The Black Cup*. "Everybody must be at the movies" one of the employees said as she turned to me. As we were heading out the door, Roy came out of his office. "Bye guys, see you in a month" he said as he waved. We walked back to the hotel and went to the main office to pay our bill. We drove to the airport and looked for a flight to Shanghai. The next flight wasn't until early morning.

We had to wait in the airport all night, so we went to a restaurant called *Plane Food*. We walked in and found a booth at the back. "Hello, my name is Dave and I will be your server this evening. Can I start you off with some drinks?" he asked. "Two waters with lime" I said. "Great and are you guys ready to order?" he asked. "I'm ready, are you ready?" I asked Kara as I looked at her.

"I will have the lasagna with garlic bread" she said. "And I will have the steak with potatoes" I said. "Great choices" he said as he wrote our orders down. "I'll be glad once we finish this and we won't have to wonder who's coming after us next" Kara said. "Ya, you said it" I said. Dave came back with our food and placed it in front of us.

"Okay, if you need anything else just let me know" he said as he walked away. I looked at my watch. "Good, we still have lots of time to sit and eat" I said. Kara took a bite. "Wow, that is incredible" she said. "How's yours?" she asked as I took a bite. "Very good" I said. Half an hour later, Dave came back and took our plates. "How was everything? Was it all to your liking?" he asked. "Yes, everything was delicious" I said.

We headed to our terminal and waited in the chairs until our plane came. I thought that it was weird that the lady at the counter kept looking at us. I knew something was wrong and nudged Kara. "I think the lady at the counter might be a hitman" I said. "No, you're crazy, there's no way" she said. "I'm not joking, I feel it in my gut" I said. "You're just being paranoid" she said.

"Maybe you're right" I said as I tried to forget it. As it got closer to the time when we were going to take off, more and more people started to fill the chairs all around us. I looked outside and saw the plane that we were going to take land on the runway. "We are going to start boarding the plane now. Rows one through twenty please come up" the lady at the counter said.

"We are now going to board the rest of the plane, rows twenty and up" she said after a while. We stood in line behind a young couple on their honeymoon. Behind us was an older couple flying home. We handed our tickets to the lady as we walked up. "Enjoy your flight" she said as she checked our tickets.

We started walking towards the plane, when the lady turned towards us and pulled out a machine gun and started to fire. She hit the old couple in the back and they both dropped to the floor like a sack of dirt. She hit the couple in front of us in the head. Their blood splattered on us as we ran onto the plane. "Close the door" I shouted to the flight attendant as I saw the lady with the machine gun running up to the plane.

The flight attendant shut the door just in time. The lady banged on the door and pointed the gun at the flight attendant. "Tell the pilot to get going" I said as she ran up to the cockpit and opened the door. "Some lady is waving a gun outside the plane, wanting to get in" she said as the pilot started the engines.

We took our seats. "Wow, that was close" Kara said as she caught her breath. The flight attendant came to see us. "Who was that?" she asked. "It's a long story, the short version is someone wants us dead" I said. "Well, you're safe now" she said. "Ya, but for how long, there might be another hitman waiting for us when we land" Kara said.

"God, I hope not, can I get you anything to drink?" she asked. "Ya, two waters with lime please" I said. "Sorry, we don't have any lime" she said. "Just water is fine then" I said. "Okay" she said as she walked away. She came back a moment later. "There you are" she said. "Thank you" we said as she went to take the other passenger's drink orders. I looked out the window and the clouds were very dark.

"Looks like a storm coming" I said. Just then we heard thunder and saw lightning. "Folks, we might have a little turbulence when we fly into this storm, but it should only last a few moments" the pilot said over the intercom. The plane started to shake violently and the other passengers were getting scared.

The shaking got worse. "We are going to crash" one of the passengers said. "No, we're not, just try to remain calm. Take some deep breaths, it will be over soon" I said as I touched the passenger's hand. "I am going to try to drop below this storm, to see if that will give us a smoother ride" the pilot said over the intercom.

"Looks like the clouds are breaking up, so it will be smooth sailing from this moment on" he said over the intercom. Kara released her grip on the arms of her chair. "Little bit nervous were you?" I asked. "Ya, weren't you?" she asked. "A little" I replied. "Liar" she said. "You're right, I was nervous" I admitted. "We are making our final descent into Shanghai, thank you for flying *China Air*" the pilot said over the intercom.

We landed and the flight attendant opened the plane door. "Have a great day" she said as we walked past her. We waited for our luggage, once we got it, we walked outside to find a taxi. We saw a taxi on the other side of the street with no cars around it. We walked up to it and got in. "Thirty Two Zing Drive please" Kara said as he pulled away from the curb and onto the highway.

"Where are you folks from?" he asked. "Sweden, but I was born here" Kara said. "I'll be so happy when this is over" Kara said as she turned to me. "Ya, me too, I don't like living like this" I said. "What brings you guys to China, business or pleasure" the taxi driver asked. "Business" I replied. We drove for another twenty minutes and then pulled up in front of Kara's house.

"Well, here we are, Thirty Two Zing Drive. Kara handed him some money. "Thank you" she said. "Not so fast" the taxi driver said as he stuck a gun in Kara's face. I knocked it out of his hand and we both got out of the car and ran down the street.

At the end of the street we looked back and saw that the car was gone. "Damn, now he knows where we live" I said. "I doubt he'll be back" Kara said as we walked up the stairs. "Let's do some training" Kara said. "Okay" I said as I followed her to her training room. "We will work on in-tight fighting. This type of fighting is great because it makes it harder for your opponent to react" she said as she got close to me.

"Put your hands up and bring your elbows in tight against your body. When you strike, turn your hips so that you get maximum power. Elbow strikes are perfect for in-tight fighting. Turn your hips as well with the elbow strikes. No matter what technique you deliver, it is very important to turn your hip and bend your knees" she said.

"Okay, that's enough for today" she said as she looked at her watch and noticed that an hour and a half went by. "Let's sit on the floor" she said as we both sat down. "Close your eyes and focus on your breathing" she continued. "We must always be ready and not ready at the same time. We must always be playful, but serious. We must be calm and relaxed, but focused and ready to react in a millisecond" she said.

We went into the living room and Kara went to make some tea. A few minutes later she came out of the kitchen with two cups of tea. "Part of the internal training is talking about Kung Fu. By talking about it, we are able to understand it better and it gets deep into our subconscious" she said. "We can switch from in-tight fighting to distance fighting as much as we want" she continued.

"I like in-tight fighting, it feels a lot less effortless and you don't have to exert the amount of energy that you do when distance fighting" I said. "Correct, it is beautiful, when you are in-tight on your opponent, they get confused and don't know what to do" she said. Half an hour later, we both finished our tea. Kara put her empty cup down on the table. "We will go see the mafia boss tomorrow, it is safer to go see him during the day" she said.

Chapter 8
The Mafia Boss

We left Kara's house late in the morning and we drove to the mafia boss's club and parked across the street. We entered the alley and started walking down it. When we looked up, we saw snipers aimed at us. We kept walking, showing no fear. "We are here to see the mafia boss" I said to the bouncer. "What is your business here?" he asked. "We are here to settle an issue" I said as he stepped aside and motioned for us to go in.

We walked inside and walked down the middle of the club as everybody was staring at us. We saw the mafia boss sitting at the booth against the back wall. We locked eyes as we walked up to him. His bodyguards came up to us and started to search us. When they didn't find anything, they stepped aside and we sat down.

"How is it that you're still alive? Why won't you die?" the mafia boss asked. "You have two choices, one, you can call off all your hitman, leave us alone and forget that we exist. Or two, we fight and only one of us walks out of here, I leave the decision up to you" Kara said. "I don't want to have to do option two, because I don't want to hurt anyone. But, if I have to, I will do whatever it takes to end this issue" Kara continued.

The mafia boss was silent for a few moments, then started to erupt in laughter. "You, beat me? The thought of it is absurd" the mafia boss said as his four bodyguards got up and moved towards us. Kara and I stood to our feet and stepped back into a right fighting stance. Two bodyguards came at me and two at Kara. We swept both of their legs as they fell to the floor.

They got back up and two of them rushed towards me. I broke one of their legs and punched the other guy in the throat, causing him to crumble to the floor unconscious. Two of them rushed Kara, she upper-cutted one of them, sending him soaring in the air and crashing on the floor dead. The other one came at her with a knife. She took it from him and stabbed him in the throat with it.

"I hate having to kill people, but if I have no choice, I will" she said. The mafia boss showed us his hands to indicate that he was unarmed. "Look, maybe we can come to an understanding" he said. "We can and here it is, forget that we exist, let us live our lives and we will let you live yours. If I have to come back here again, I will not be so forgiving" Kara said.

As we turned to go, the mafia boss took out his gun and shot Kara in the back. I heard a body dropping to the ground, turned around and saw him holding a gun. He then pointed it at me. "It is a shame that she had to die, but nobody screws with me. I dove to the ground and crawled to safety behind a booth. He unloaded his gun in my direction. I stayed hidden as he got to his feet and walked over to the booth were I was hiding.

"Oh Ryan, come out come out wherever you are" he taunted as I crawled from one booth to the next. I jumped over the booth, ran at him and punched him in the face, followed by a kick to the groin. He grabbed his groin and fell to the ground. I kicked him in the face and he fell on his back. He had blood dripping from his face. "Go on, do it, put me out of my misery" he said as he spit blood at me.

"I'm not going to kill you, it's not what Kara would have wanted. I am going to have you locked up for a long time" I said. "I'll be seeing you real soon" he said as the police came, hand cuffed him and took him down to the police station. I ran over to Kara and held her. I turned her over and she was still alive. "I love you Ryan" she said as her eyes closed for good. "Nooooooo" I yelled in agony. I picked her body up and walked out of the club.

I drove back to her house and dug a grave in the backyard and placed her in it. "My love and my teacher, I will miss you more than words can explain. You became the best part of me, you will always be in my heart all the days of my life" I said as I shoveled dirt onto her body.

Tears were gushing down my face as I walked back in the house. I made myself her favorite tea and drank it out in the backyard.

I went over in my mind all the good times that we had. I had a hard time believing that she was gone, it all happened so fast. I couldn't help but think, what if there were more hitman that he hired? I had to be on the lookout still, I didn't know who I could trust.

I needed to get away from the house for a while, so I went for a walk. I started to walk down the sidewalk and walked all night. On my way back, I stopped to sit on a bench that overlooked the river. A beautiful woman sat down right beside me. "I heard about Kara, I'm sorry" she said. "Who are you?" I asked. "My name is Natally and I was a friend of Kara" she said. "How did you know she is dead?" I asked. "This is Shanghai, word spreads fast around here" she said.

I got up and started to walk back. "Let me come with you" she said. "Okay, sure" I replied. We talked about her all the way back to the house. She told me stories about her that I didn't even know. I told her stories that she didn't know. We reached the front steps to the house. "Would you like to come in, I buried her in the backyard, you can say some words" I said.

"Ya, I would like to" she said as we both walked in the house. "Tea?" I asked. "Oh, yes please" she replied. I poured the tea and we both walked out to the backyard. "Kara was a good friend and good friends are hard to find, I'll miss you Kara, I love you" she said as she teared up. We sat down and drank our tea. "Where do you live?" I asked.

"On the other side of town" she answered. When we finished our tea, we got into the car and I drove her home. "Listen, if you ever need to talk or you want a friend, I'll be here for you" she said as she gave me her phone number. "Thanks" I said as she got out and walked up to her house. She turned and waved at me as she went inside.

On the drive home, I was thinking about when I should go back to Sweden. Something wouldn't let me leave. I didn't know what it was, I felt drawn to stay here. I walked in the door, I was so tired that I fell asleep right away. The next morning, I got woken up by singing birds that were sitting on the window ledge. After my morning tea, I went out for a walk along the river.

The pathway was littered with people walking in every direction. I heard a couple shots and saw a couple of people around me drop to the ground. I dropped to the ground and crawled to a safe location. I looked all around, on the tops of buildings, but I couldn't see anyone. I waited in a safe spot for hours. I didn't know how many shooters there were or if they could see me.

I decided to run for it, I scrambled to my feet and ran as fast as I could. Bullets were landing inches away from my feet, but I kept running until I got behind a cement barrier. I figured that there was only one shooter, because the bullets only came from one direction. I looked again to see if I could see who I was dealing with.

The shooter started shooting again. I saw the shots coming from the tenth floor of a building that was facing the river. I was determined to get to that building. I ran and snuck in the back. I took the elevator up to the tenth floor and searched every room until I found the one he was in. I waited until it sounded like he was out of bullets. I kicked the door down and ran up to him.

He turned around just as I threw a kick. I hit him in the chest, sending him flying back and he crashed through the window. I walked up to see if he was dead, but I found him hanging on to the window frame. He was slipping and I grabbed his hand. "How many more are after me?" I asked. "How many?" I yelled. He fell and his body splattered blood on the sidewalk below.

I started walking back to the house. A man walked up to me and when he was a few feet away from me, he pulled a knife and tried to stab me. I took the knife from him and held it to his throat. "Alright, how many more are after me?" I asked. "Three, I think" he said as he shook with fear. He swept me with his leg. I fell to the ground and he held the knife to my throat.

"I have a message for you, the boss says that he is going to get out of jail real soon. And when he does, he is going to track you down and kill you" he said. I grabbed the knife with my hand and I stuck it in his forehead. I rolled him off me and as I was breathing heavily, I was on the lookout for anyone else while I walked the rest of the way home.

I decided to call Natally. I picked up the phone and dialed. "Hi Natally, it's Ryan, would you like to come over and have some tea?" I asked. "Sure, I would love to, it might take me a long time to get there because I have to walk" she said. "I'll come pick you up in the car" I said.

"Great, I'll see you in a little while" she said as she hung up the phone. I drove to her house and saw her standing on the front porch. She locked her front door and got in the car. "I'm glad you called me" she said. "Really? Why?" I asked. "I thought you might need someone to talk to" she said.

We pulled up and went inside. We walked into the kitchen and I made some tea for us. We walked out to the backyard with our tea. "So, how did you know Kara?" I asked. "We went to the same Kung Fu school together" she said. "Really? Wow" I said. "Why, how did you know her?" she asked. "She got me to come to her dad's Kung Fu school, then when he died, she became my teacher and we took over his school" I said.

"That's fascinating, let's see your skills" she said as she stood up and got into a stance. I stood up and got into a stance as well. She threw the first punch and I blocked it. I retaliated and we sparred for a good hour, trading blow after blow. "Kara trained you well" Natally said. We sat down and talked about internal training concepts.

"What are your plans now?" she asked. "I'm going to go back to Sweden" I said. "Maybe I can come with you and we can teach at the school together" she said. "I'll have to think about it" I said. "I am going to stay here for a few days, so I'll let you know" I said as I got up and started to walk to the front door.

"I'll give you a lift to your house" I said as I grabbed my keys. "Okay" she said as she followed me out the door. We got in the car and drove off. I walked her up her stairs to her door and she gave me a kiss on the cheek. "Thanks for the ride" she said as she went inside.

I pulled up to the front of Kara's house, got out and went inside. I was so tired that I went straight to bed. I tossed and turned thinking about Natally. A bunch of thoughts were racing through my mind. What if she was a hitman for the mafia boss? What if she was Kara's daughter? Could I trust her? Should I allow her to teach in the school with me? Finally after an hour, I fell asleep.

I dreamed that Kara was alive and we were on a beach, with our kids running around. I awoke to the sound of a tree smacking its branches against the window in my room. I got out of bed and went to the window. The wind was blowing hard and heavy rain was pouring down. I got back in bed, shut my eyes and tried to fall asleep again. I had another dream about Kara and this time my family was in it.

I was so excited to see them, I went up to them and kissed and hugged them. I opened my eyes and the sun was shining in through the window. I looked over at the clock. "Wow, I slept in" I said. I put on my sweatpants, got my tea and went and sat out in the backyard. It was a beautiful morning, the birds were chirping and the sun was shining down on my face. There was a nice, light breeze in the air. I thought about when I would go back to Sweden and I thought about how I was going to tell my students about what happened.

I went out for a walk after I finished my tea. I walked down to the market. I stopped to buy some fruit, I picked out what I wanted and went to pay for it. I handed the man some money and all of a sudden, I heard three shots and blood started pouring out of his chest. I ducked and ran to safety behind a car. More shots were fired into the side of the car and I ran to the next car as I dropped the fruit.

I needed to get out of there or I would be dead. I waited until I thought he was reloading. I stayed low and ran down the street. Bullets hit the ground as I ran for my life. I made it to the end of the street and hid behind a building. "These shooters are everywhere" I said as I looked around for more. I didn't see any, so I carefully walked home.

"Hi Ryan, just phoning to see how you are making out" Natally said over the phone. "It is rough, I got shot at today while I was at the market" I said. "Really? Did you see who it was?" she asked. "No, I was just concerned about getting the hell out of there" I replied. "Come pick me up and we'll talk about it" she said as I hung up the phone and drove to her house.

She opened the car door, got in and we drove back to the house. We sat outside with our cup of tea. "So, have you decided when you are going back to Sweden?" she asked. "Ya, I want to leave tonight" I said. "Can I come with you?" she asked. "I've been thinking about that, my answer is yes, you can come" I said.

"Great" she said as she hugged me. She jumped up and down clapping her hands. "I'll have to drive you back home on the way to the airport so that you can pack a bag" I said. "What about you? Are you going to start packing?" she asked. "I've already packed" I said.

I drove her to her house. "Make sure you pack warm clothes, it is going to be cold"

I said. "You can come in with me if you want" she said. "Okay" I said as I followed her in. Twenty minutes later we walked out the front door with her carrying a suitcase. "Throw it in the trunk" I said as I popped the trunk open and she threw it in.

We drove down her block, we reached the highway and had to stop. Traffic was backed up all the way from the airport. I looked in the mirror and saw a car speeding towards us on the shoulder lane. "We have to move" I said as I pushed my way through the sea of cars. I got onto the shoulder lane and punched the gas.

The other car was on our tail, but I managed to stay ahead of him. I tried to lose him by cutting through the sea of cars again. I cranked the wheel and bashed car after car to get to the other side. "Do you see him?" I asked as I looked in the mirror and saw that he was right behind me.

He began to fire his gun and shot the back windshield. Natally grabbed the top of her head and screamed. We sped past a police car, he turned on his lights and started chasing us. He got in the middle of my car and the other car.

The car that was chasing us smashed into the police car, sending the police car spinning out of control. The police car flipped four times before coming to a stop. He continued to shoot at us and shot off both of our rear view mirrors. We sped past two more police cars and they joined the chase.

They were behind the car that was chasing us. They fired their shotgun and shot out the hitman's back windshield. They shot again and hit a hitman siting in the passenger side. The driver sped up and smashed into us. We weaved from left to right, almost flipping. The driver suddenly slammed on his brakes, causing the police cars to crash into the back of them.

They flipped over onto their hoods as the hitman sped off after us. They slammed into us again, we spun around so we were looking right at him. He shot at us and missed. "Look in the glove compartment" I said. "Why?" she asked. "Just do it" I yelled. She opened it up and took out a gun. "Shoot him" I said as she stuck the gun out the window and shot.

He moved and the bullet went through the head rest. She shot again and the bullet hit him in the right arm. He had to switch hands while driving. She shot the hood of the car. It exploded, flipped over our car and crashed behind us. I spun around and continued to the airport. "Are you okay? Are you hit? I asked. "No, I'm fine" she answered. "Are you fine?" she asked. "Yes" I replied. We returned to the congested traffic. "That was scary" she said. "Tell me about it" I said.

Another car barreled towards us, sending cars flying left and right. "Drive" she screamed. I gunned the car in reverse and sped off using the side lane. "What is with these guy?" I asked. Two machine guns popped out each side of their car and they began shooting at us. A police helicopter was flying overhead with a sniper aboard.

The sniper took aim and shot the car's gas tank. The guys with the machine guns turned their attention to the helicopter and shot at it. The helicopter started to smoke and crashed to the ground with a massive explosion. The explosion blew up five cars that were in traffic. The hitman sped up, they were right on our tail. "Take the wheel" I said as I leaned out the window with the gun and shot at their tires.

I hit the front driver's tire and it went flat, causing their car to spray sparks all down the road. I grabbed a brick from the back of the car and chucked it at the hitman's car. It hit the car and flipped it nine times before starting on fire. They tried to get out, but the car blew up. We drove off and finally made it to the airport.

"When is your next flight to Sweden?" I asked the girl behind the counter. "We have one leaving right now, if you hurry, you can make it" she said. "Great" I said. We bought two tickets and we ran to the gate. "Wait, hold it" I yelled as we ran up just as the lady was closing the door to the jet way. "Hurry" she said as we gave her the tickets, ran onto the plane and took our seats.

"There was a moment there where I thought we were done for" she said. "You're a great driver" she continued. "Thanks" I replied. "Wake me up when we get there" she said as she closed her eyes. "Okay" I said. I took out my book, *how to deal with the mafia* and started reading. I put it down a while later and closed my eyes. Before I knew it, I was asleep. I woke up half an hour later and walked to the bathroom.

A flight attendant saw me go in, waited a minute and followed me. She opened the door and pulled out a knife. "You can run, but you can't hide" she said as she lunged at me with the knife. I tossed her to the back wall, her head hit the toilet, knocking her unconscious. I walked out.

"What is with these people?" I asked myself as I sat down. Natally opened her eyes and looked at me. "Is everything okay?" she asked. "Great" I replied. "Just a little unpleasantness in the bathroom" I continued. "Ya, airline food will do that to you" she said as she shut her eyes again.

When she opened our eyes again, we were starting to land. We grabbed our bag from overtop of us and walked off the plane. We walked out the front door of the airport and walked to Kara's car that was parked in the long term parking lot. I started crying when we saw the car. "What's wrong Ryan?" she asked. "I'm just thinking about Kara and how much I miss her" I replied. She put her arm around me. "I miss her too" she said.

I drove to Kara's home. "So this was Kara's home?" she asked. "Yes" I replied. "It's beautiful" she said as we walked up the steps. I unlocked the door and we went in. "Later I'll show you the school that used to belong to Kara's dad" I said. "Make yourself at home" I said as she sat down on the couch and put her feet up. Later that night we walked *to The Dark Panther*.

I made a sign and put it in the window. *The Dark Panther will be open starting August fifteenth in the morning for meditation, I expect to see all of my students there.* I brought her into the office. "I thought that maybe you would like to help teach" I said.

"Ya, I would love to" she replied. "Great" I said. "So, we have meditation a few mornings a week and class is every night" I continued. She sat at Kara's old desk and I showed her the schedule. "I'll introduce you to the students when we open" I said.

We walked in the door of *The Black Cup*. We walked behind the counter and into a small office. "Hi Roy" I said. "Ryan, how the hell are you?" he asked. "Doing okay" I said. "Roy, this is Natally, she would like a job here" I said. "Where's Kara?" he asked as my eyes darted to the floor. "She died" I said. "Holy shit Ryan, I am so sorry to hear that" he said.

"Ya, of course she can work here, just fill out this application" he said as he handed it to her. "Thanks Roy" I said as we sat down at a booth and she filled it out. "Would you guys like a coffee?" he yelled. "Ya, two coffees would be great" I said. "Coming right up" he said. A few moments later he came over to our table and handed us two coffees.

"Thanks Roy" I said. "Here you go" Natally said as she handed her application to Roy. "Thanks, I will enter you into the system and you can start tomorrow with Ryan" he said. We opened the door and walked home. On the way, we saw two men attacking a woman. I started to head their direction, but Natally grabbed my arm. "Where are you going?" she asked.

"I'm going to help her" I said. "Leave it alone" she said. "I can't do that" I said as I went up to the men. "What the hell are you guys doing?" I asked. "Scram asshole, this is none of your concern" one of the guys said. "Ya, well I'm making it my concern" I said.

"Oh, a tough guy eh" the other guy said. They both walked up to me with baseball bats. One of them swung at me, I flowed with the bat and took it from him and punched him in the throat. He dropped to the ground gasping for air.

The other guy took out his knife and slashed at me. I grabbed the knife and stabbed him in the leg. "Thank you so much sir, how can I ever repay you?" the woman asked. "Just knowing that you're okay is enough thanks for me" I said as she kissed me on the lips and ran home.

"Why didn't you help?" I asked. "Because, that is not my concern" she replied. "Why did you help?" she asked. "Because they would have killed her" I said. "So what if they did?" she asked. "I don't want to see any innocent person killed, if I can help save a life, I will" I said.

"You can sleep in my bed, I'll sleep on the couch" I said as we got back to the house. "We need to be up early for morning meditation at *The Dark Panther*" I said. "Okay" she said as she walked upstairs. We got to *The Dark Panther* really early. We both sat down and started meditating. It was silent for twenty minutes before the students started to pour in.

"Great to see each and every one of you again" I said. "This is Natally, she will be helping me teach, she is one of Kara's students" I continued. "Where is Kara?" Windy asked. "Kara is dead, she died tragically in Shanghai" I said as the whole school went silent for a few moments. "I will hold a memorial for her tonight, if anyone wants to say a few words about her" I continued.

We were in the office as all the students left. "How did you get so many students to join your school?" she asked. "Kara and I took an advertisement out in the paper" I said. "That was clever" she replied. I went over to her desk. "Here are the fees from the students from last month. I need you to count to see if the amount is the same as the one on their signed form" I said as I handed her a pile.

"Okay" she said. I sat down and started to prepare the lesson that I was going to teach later on. We stayed at *The Dark Panther* all afternoon until it was time to go to work. "First day of work, are you excited?" I asked as we started to leave. I locked the door behind her. "Ya, this will be fun, working with you, plus teaching Kung Fu with you" she said.

"Here is your uniform, go in the back, change and then come back out front. I want you to shadow Ryan and the rest" Roy said as he handed her a uniform. She came out and everyone introduced themselves to her. A line up started to form and I could see her getting overwhelmed.

I took her by the hand and looked into her eyes. "Don't worry about all the people, just do your best" I said as I walked back to taking the customers' orders. The last customer left and she went out to the lobby to sweep as I walked up to her. "Great job tonight Natally" I said. I headed back behind the counter to cash out the register.

I unlocked the front door to *The Dark Panther* and we went to the office. A few moments later the students started to come in. They got changed and then waited in the lobby for us. We came out a moment later. "I have prepared a small lesson and then towards the end of class, if anyone wants to say anything about Kara, they can" I said.

Natally and I are going to stand here and anyone who wants to spar with us are welcome to. Everyone was silent for a few moments, then Windy walked up to me. "I will spar with you" she said. "Okay great" I said as we both started. "Slow it down" I said as she was throwing fast punches. Health walked up to Natally, got into his circle stance and began sparring with her.

One after the other, they came up to spar with us for a few moments. "Great job guys, you're coming along nicely" I said as we stopped. "If anyone would like to say something about Kara, do it now" I said as I stepped back. "You were an amazing teacher and we are going to miss you very much" Fay said. "You taught us many life lessons and were very warm and kind" Susie said.

"You touched our hearts, not only as a teacher, but as a friend" Chip said. "Your memory will live on and you will always be in our thoughts" Kristy said. One by one, all of the students came up and said something about Kara. "Okay guys, that is it for tonight, no meditation class tomorrow.

See you all back here tomorrow night. I want you to practice your stances and circle walking" I said as they all went to the change rooms. I locked the door behind the last student. "You really care about your students don't you?" Natally asked. "Of course I do, they are a part of me and I am a part of them" I said.

Chapter 9
Deception

We walked in the house very late. "I have to tell you something Ryan" Natally said. "Okay, I'm listening" I said. "Let's go in the family room, I will make us some tea" she said as she went in the kitchen and boiled some water. She came out a few moments later with two green teas. She handed me one and sat down. "What is it?" I asked. "Okay, I am a hitman for the mafia boss and I was sent to kill you, but I fell in love with you" she said.

I was silent for a while. "I knew there was something fishy about you" I said as I reached for my sword. She grabbed my hand. "Stop, I am not going to kill you, I like you a lot, but I understand if you never want to see me again" she said as she dropped her head.

"I like you too, but your loyalty is to the mafia boss, how am I able to trust you?" I asked. "Because I could have killed you anytime I wanted, but I didn't, doesn't that count for something?" she replied. "I guess so" I said. "Look, whatever you decide, just know that I love you and I don't want anything to happen to you" she said.

I got up and started to walk to the door. "Where are you going?" she asked. "I have to think about things" I said. "Oh, okay, I understand" she said as I shut the door behind me. "How could I have been so stupid? I had a feeling that she was a hitman" I said to myself. I thought about what I was going to do. I thought about if I was going to kick her out of the house or let her stay.

I mean, she works for the mafia boss, how could I trust her? But then why would she tell me this, was she just playing with me? Or was she being honest and sincere? I walked up and down the streets and the alleys trying to come up with a solution to this issue. I walked up to the front door and walked in. Natally got up from the couch. "I am glad you're back" she said.

"I have thought long and hard about this. The fact is that you're a hitman for the mafia boss. But you were honest with me and I kept on thinking, why would she tell me if she was going to kill me? Maybe you told me because you don't want to kill me" I said. "Does this mean I can stay?" she asked. "Yes, you can stay" I said. "Oh thank you, thank you" she replied as she kissed me on the lips.

We went out to the backyard and did some training. A while later we came back in and went up to bed. "Can I sleep with you tonight?" she asked. "Okay" I said as she climbed into bed with me. We woke up in the middle of the night to the door bell ringing. "Stay here, I will find out what's going on" I said as I went downstairs and opened the door.

Two police men were standing there. "Sorry to bother you sir, but do you own a blue mini cooper?" one of them asked. "Yes, I do" I answered. "Sorry to tell you this sir, but it's been incinerated" he said. "Really? When? How?" I asked. "We don't know, we just saw it on fire and ran the license plate and it came back to you" he said.

"Damn, I loved that car" I said as I started to shut the door. "Wait, there's more" he said as he handed me a note. I opened up the note and the words *you're next* were written on it. "What does it say?" the other police man asked. "It is just my grocery list" I lied as I shut the door and walked upstairs.

"Is everything okay?" Natally asked I climbed back into bed. "No, my mini cooper was incinerated and there was a note that said *you're next*. "Oh no, do you have any idea who did it?" she asked. "I have one idea" I said. "What is it?" she asked. "I'm thinking it was another hitman who works for the mafia boss" I said. "No, it can't be" she replied. "Then who do you think did it? It was no coincidence" I said.

We went back inside and walked upstairs. I fell asleep and dreamt of the mafia boss. I dreamt that he rang the doorbell, I walked downstairs, opened it and he shot me four times in the chest with his pp7 silencer.

He walked upstairs, kicked the bedroom door in and shot Natally two times in the head. He walked back downstairs and saw that I was still alive. He took out his knife and stabbed me in the back. I sat up screaming as sweat dripped from my face.

"What is it Ryan?" she asked. "I had a dream that the mafia boss killed us both" I said. "You can rest peacefully knowing that he is in jail and will probably die in there" she said. "Wait, how do you know he's in jail?" I asked. "Because you told me" she answered. "Oh ya that's right, I did" I replied. I laid back down and shut my eyes.

The next morning, we got ourselves some tea and went out to the backyard. We sat and meditated, the chirping of the birds was peaceful to our ears. Every once in a while we would say something to each other, like, I feel the wind on my arms or I feel the warmth of the sun on my face. We opened our eyes up half an hour later.

"I feel so good" I said. "Me too" she said. "I can't help shake the feeling that the mafia boss will get out of jail" I said. "You're just being paranoid" she said. "Ya, you might be right" I replied. We got up and started to spar. We started off slow and sped up. "Have you been practicing?" she asked. "Yes I have" I answered. "It shows" she replied. We sparred for half an hour. "Alright, that's enough, I need some water" Natally said as we went in and got some water.

We walked in the door of *The Black Cup*, went to the back and changed into our uniforms. As we headed up to the counter, we saw Roy, he was limping. "What's wrong Roy?" I asked. "I got mugged last night walking home" he said. "Oh no, that's awful" Natally said. "They stole my wallet and kicked me in the leg, thank god they didn't break it" Roy said.

"Are you okay?" I asked. "I am better now" he said. "Don't worry about me, I'll be alright" he said. We went up to the counter and took over for the others who left. "Welcome to *The Black Cup*" Natally said as a customer approached her. "What can I get for you?" she asked.

"You can start by giving me all the money in the register" he said as he held a knife to her throat. She didn't flinch. "Aren't you scared?" he asked. "No, I'm not" she replied. "Why not?" he asked. "Because" she said. "Because why?" he asked. "Because I know that you are too much of a coward to hurt me" she answered.

His knife started to shake. "Oh, be careful" she said. "You don't want to cut me" she continued. "Just give me the bloody money" he said. She knew that any move could cost her her life. "Here you go" she said as she handed the money over to him in a bag. He turned and ran out the door. Roy came running out, having seen it take place on the surveillance camera. "Good job Natally, you did the right thing, not taking matters into your own hands" he congratulated her.

The rest of our shift was slow, the big line up of customers that we did have was scared away when that guy pulled his knife. Roy phone the police and they came right away. Natally gave them a description of what the guy was wearing, his age and what color of hair he had. They left and searched the streets for him.

"Quite a night hey?" Roy asked as we were heading out the door. "Ya, it was something else" Natally replied. We walked across the road to *The Dark Panther*. We walked in and sat down in our office just as the students started to arrive. "Well, looks like we better get out there" I said as we stood up. "Tonight I want you guys to do some sparring with each other as Natally and I walk around the room" I said as they began to pair up.

The night went by fast, before we knew it, it was time to go home. "Great work guys" Natally said. "Go home and practice punching in front of a mirror" I said. "As you may have seen on the schedule, there's not going to be meditation tomorrow" Natally said. They all headed to the change rooms and then left. We went back to the office to work on the next lesson.

I locked the door behind her and we started to walk home. "What was that like, having a knife held at your throat?" I asked. "It was not pleasant, but it has happened before" she said. "Where? When?" I asked. "Back in China, a guy pulled a knife on me because he wanted my taxi" I said. "That was great, you were so calm" I said. "Ya, I looked into his eyes and saw that he didn't want to hurt me" she answered.

When we got to the front steps, I found a note, it read, *you're next*. "What the hell? Not again, is this some kind of joke?" I asked. "Let me see" Natally said as I handed her the note. "Who did this?" she asked. "I don't know" I said. "But I am going to find out" I continued. "How are you going to do that? You don't even know where to start" she said. "I will meditate on it, eventually I'll find out who it is" I said.

We walked inside and went and sat outside in the backyard. We talked for an hour about what we were going to teach in our next lesson. "It's late, let's go up to bed" I said as I stood up and started walking inside as Natally followed. "Do you think it is one of our students that wrote the notes?" she asked. "No, I don't think so" I replied. "I hope you don't have any nightmares tonight" Natally said. "Me too" I said. "Well goodnight" I said as I kissed her and shut my eyes.

I woke up early the next morning. I carefully climbed out of bed so that I wouldn't wake Natally. I went out to the backyard, I sat on the grass and meditated. I heard footsteps behind me. "Good morning honey, here you go" Natally said as she handed me a cup of coffee. I got up and we sat on chairs. "Any lucky hunches about who you think wrote those notes?" she asked. "No, nothing yet" I replied.

"Don't worry, you will" she said. We heard a knock on the front door. We went to open it up and saw Melisa standing there. "Hello Natally, hello Ryan" she said. "Hi Melisa, what are you doing here?" Natally asked. "I was wondering if I could get a private lesson from either of you?" she asked. "Yes of course, come on in" I said. "We will go to the backyard" I said. "Do you want anything to drink?" Natally asked.

"Water please" she said. "Okay, I will go get it" Natally said as she went back in the house. She came back out with two glasses of water. "I thought you might want one too dear" she said. "Thanks babe" I said. "Was there anything in particular that you wanted to work on?" I asked. "Ya, I was having trouble with my heel thrust kicks" Melisa said. "Okay, we'll start with that" I said.

"Get into your left fighting stance" I said as I got into mine. "Raise your knee all the way up to your hip like this" I said as I demonstrated. "Then thrust the bottom of your heel down and out, like this" I said as I demonstrated. "Like this?" she asked. "Kinda, but you have to raise your knee higher and really put some power behind your thrust" I continued.

She tried and tried. "I'll never get it" she said. "Sure you will, it just takes lots of practice" I reassured her. "Try again" I said as she did it exactly how I told her to. "There you go, that was awesome" I said as she smiled. "Let's do a few more of those and then we will do the heel thrust kick from the right fighting stance" I said as she nodded. "Okay, well, keep practicing that" I said.

"Anything else you need help with?" I asked. "Ya, I am struggling with the circle walking" she said. "Okay, let me show you, Natally would you join us?" I asked. "Sure" she said as she walked over. "Okay watch, Natally and I will demonstrate" I said as we started to walk the circle. "We are walking the circle with the left side in" Natally said. "When walking the circle going left, you lead with your left foot and your right foot steps ahead of your left" she continued.

"You turn your right foot inwards slightly to stay on an imaginary circle, like this" I said as both Natally and I showed her. "Why don't you give it a shot?" Natally asked. "Okay" Melisa said as she followed behind us in the circle, trying to copy our every move. "Good job" Natally said. "Now, in order to make your walk flow, you want to land down on your heel with each step you take.

When you bring your foot up to move it, you want to roll up on the toe, like this" I said as we showed her. She tried to do it. "Almost, but when you land down on the heel, roll your weight forward, like this" I said as we showed her. "Like this?" she asked as she showed us. "Exactly, you are getting the hang of it" Natally said. "The more you practice, the smoother you will become" I said.

"Now, we are going to walk the circle with the right side in. Like you might have guessed, you lead with your right foot. The left foot steps next and ends up behind. You toe in with the right foot so that you don't get off track of the circle" I said as we showed her. "You want your heel to land down and then you want to roll onto it, just like the left circle walking" Natally said.

"You also want to come up on the toe with the other foot" I said. "Like this?" she asked as she showed us. "You got it" I said. We walked the circle for another half an hour. "Okay, let's sit down and have some tea" Natally said as she went in the house and poured tea for all of us. She came out a few moments later and handed a cup of tea to us. We sat there and looked at the trees for a moment.

"Circle walking is great for improving your balance" I said. "It also calms the mind" Natally said. "From the circle, you can do everything that you can do from a fighting stance position" I said. "When you are in a fight, it will confuse your opponent, he won't know how to track you" Natally said. "What happens if your opponent knows circle walking?" she asked. "Then you do a tighter circle around him. Later in class, we will talk about tight and wide circles". I said.

We walked her to the front door. "Thanks for the lesson, it really helped" she said. "You're welcome" we said as we shut the door behind her. We walked back outside and sat down in our chairs. "I thought she did very well" I said. "I did too, she will get even better with time and practice" Natally said.

"I thought that tonight we could do some more circle walking with the students. Then I was thinking we would talk about Kung Fu and let them ask questions" I said. "That sounds great, let's do it" Natally said. We both sat there for a while listening to the birds. We felt the wind as it blew through our hair and against our faces.

That night at work it was so slow, there were next to no customers. Natally and I kept our eye on the clock, which seemed to move incredibly slowly. When we closed, we didn't have to sweep the lobby, due to the fact that there was no customers to create a mess. We got changed and headed out the door to *The Dark Panther*. We unlocked the door and headed into the office.

We were interrupted by the sound of students coming in through the doors and heading to the change rooms. When they got out of the change rooms, they saw that Natally and I were ready to teach and they all gathered around us. "We are going to do more circle walking tonight, so what I want you guys to do is, to form a circle" I said.

The students formed a circle. "Not so big" I said as they tightened up the circle. "I am going to start with my left side in" I said as I walked inside the students. Notice how when I walk I am landing on the heel and coming up on the toe" I said.

"I am bringing my hands up. Notice how as I walk the circle my hands are always facing the middle. I don't want my hands to lose sight of the middle or my opponent" I said. "When I do an inside change, I roll on my heel and change my hand positions" I said as I showed them. I stopped. "Who would like to give it a try?" I asked.

Joy put up her hand. "Okay Joy, come on in and lead with your left side in" I said. She started walking. "Good, good" I said. "Remember, land on the heel and roll up on the toe" I said. "Now do an inside change and walk the other way" I said as she did it. "Great, keep practicing, I want smoothness in your walk and when you land on your heel" I said as she walked back to her spot in the circle.

"Anyone else?" Natally asked. Bridget raised her hand and started to walk the circle with her left side in. "Get those hands up" Natally said. "Never drop your hands. When you drop your hands, you are giving an opening to your opponent and he will take it" she said. "Good job Bridget, you can go back" I said.

"Who's next?" I asked as Jessica stepped forward and started to walk the circle. "No, left side circle walking, not right" I said as she changed and walked the other way. "Keep your back straight, don't hunch over" I said. "Great, now change" I said as she changed to right circle walking. "Remember roll on the heel" I said.

"Next" Natally said as April came forward. "Don't look down at your feet, look straight ahead" she said. Your feet know where they are, you need to keep your eyes on your opponent" she continued. "Good job, you can go back" I said. A few more of the students came up and tried walking the circle. "Okay, let's all sit down and discuss what we're learning and if you have any questions, you can ask them" Natally said.

Natally and I sat down as the rest of the class followed and we began to talk. "Kung Fu will affect every area of your life, every situation and every circumstance that you go through. You will be thinking and acting from Kung Fu" I said. "You will become so focused, so disciplined, that other people won't even recognize you" Natally said. "Kung Fu will build you into a strong, determined person, you will be trained not to quit" I said.

"Now, we will open the floor up for discussion" Natally said. "I notice that when I walk the circle, I am focused and calm" Cheer said. "Yes, the circle is an excellent tool to calm the mind and focus the thoughts" Natally said. "When I am practicing, it feels like nothing on earth exists" Kate said as some of the others nodded. "I know, isn't that cool?" I asked as she nodded. "Not only is Kung Fu good for focus, but it also is a great stress reliever" Natally said.

"Any questions that you would like to ask Nataly or I?" I asked. "How much should we be practicing?" Pretty asked. "A little bit every day, if you can't do that, then at least twice a week" Nataly answered. "When are you considered a master?" Rob asked. "I like to think that you are only considered a master when you die, because then you can't learn any more" I replied.

The students spent the next twenty minutes asking questions and we answered them. "Okay, great work tonight guys, there will be no meditation class again tomorrow" Nataly said. "Jeff, can I see you in my office" I asked. A few moments later he walked into our office.

"Jeff, you still owe the fees for this month" I said. "Oh ya, I totally forgot to give them to you, I have them in my bag, I'll go get it" he said as he went to the change room. He got the fees from the side pocket of his bag and walked back into the office.

"Here you go" he said as he handed me his fees. "Thank you" I said. "You're welcome" he replied as he left. I walked outside our office and waved at the students as they walked out the door. Natally and I went back into our office, sat down and I started to flip through Jeff's money to check if it was all there. A note fell onto my desk as I was flipping through the money. It was a grocery list, I held it up and studied it.

"What is it?" Natally asked. "Another threatening note?" she asked. "It's a grocery list from Jeff" I said. "So" Natally said. "I know I've seen this writing before" I said. I looked at it for a while. "Of course, it is the same hand writing as those threatening notes" I said.

"I am going to have a talk with Jeff tomorrow" I said. "Aren't you afraid?" Natally asked. "Of what? Of Jeff?" I asked. "No" I said. "He should be afraid of me. I'll get to the bottom of why he wrote those notes to me" I continued. "I can't believe that was him who wrote those notes" Natally said as she shook her head. Natally and I counted the rest of the students fees, it took us two hours.

"Okay, everyone is paid up for this month" I said. Natally and I grabbed our coats, walked out the front door as I locked it behind her. "What if those notes were just meant to be a joke?" she asked. "What kind of sick joke is that?" I asked. "I'll just wait until I talk to him, I don't want to jump to any conclusions" I said as I yawned. We reached the front steps and I opened the door. We went into the kitchen and turned on the tea kettle.

"Was that always there?" Natally asked as she pointed to a note on the table. "No, that one's new, I have the other notes upstairs" I said as I picked it up. It had the same words on it as the other ones. We heard footsteps as I ran to see who was there. A dark shadow ran out the back door and vanished into the night. I chased the shadow, but he was too fast.

I ran to the end of the block, bent down and picked up a piece of his jeans that got ripped when he jumped the fence. "Did you get him?" Natally asked when I got back to the house. "No, all I found was this and it doesn't tell me anything" I said as I threw the fabric down on the floor.

The next morning I stretched my arm out in bed to find that Natally was gone. I walked to the window and saw her in the backyard meditating. I felt like I needed to give her some space, so I waited a while before bringing coffee out for both of us. I sat down beside her, didn't say a word, I just put a coffee beside her. I closed my eyes and we sat in silence for a while. "Thanks for the coffee" she said with her eyes still closed.

"I'm thinking that we should buy another car" she continued. "What do you think?" she asked. "What kind do you want?" she asked. "I want a Mustang Super Snake" I said. "Okay, let's go get it" she said as we went inside and headed out. A few hours later we pulled up in front of the house in a brand new blue Mustang Super Snake.

We drove it to work that evening. "Wow, is that your guys' car?" Roy asked. "Sure is" I said. "That's nice" he said. "Thanks" Natally said. Work was so busy, it felt like we only worked for ten minutes. We left and went to *The Dark Panther*. "I will talk to Jeff after class" I said to Natally while we were in the office. One by one, the students started to come through the door and went to the change rooms.

"With me today, I have brought some hand pads so we can practice our punching" I said. "I want everyone to line up. I will hold the pads and I want you to do two punches to the chest and one to the lower body" I said as I held the pads up to my chest. One by one the students came up to me, punched the pads and walked to the end of the line. I gave the pads to Natally.

"This time I don't want any tension in your arms, I want you to relax" she said. The last student finished and went to the back of the line. "Good job guys" she said. "I still want even less tension in those arms" she continued. "Much better everyone" she said as the last student walked back.

"I want you now to do a toe snap kick and go" I said as I held one of the pads facing down. "Bring your knee up higher and just throw the foot" I said as Energy walked away. "Good work tonight, that is the end of class, see you all here for meditation tomorrow morning" Natally said.

"Jeff, can I talk to you for a moment?" I asked. "Ya, sure" he said as he followed me to my office. I shut the door. "You are doing great, you're coming along nicely" I said. "Thank you" Jeff said. "One thing that I am concerned about is, I have been receiving these threatening notes that say *you're next*. And the other day when you gave me the fee money, I was counting it and a grocery list fell out. I looked at it and realized that it matches the writing on those threatening notes that I received.

Do you know anything about that?" I asked. He reached into his pocket and pulled out a gun. As he was raising it above my desk, I saw it, knocked it out of his hand and punched him in the throat. He dropped to the floor with a thud. A moment later, he came to his senses and ran out of the office, past Natally and out of the building. He left so fast that he forgot his gun. I picked it up and put it in the first drawer of my desk.

"What was that all about?" Natally asked as she walked in the office and sat at her desk. "Jeff pulled a gun on me" I said. "No way" she said. "Way" I said. "So what's your next move?" she asked. "Well, I'm going to expel him from the school and we better be on the lookout.

Because I think that he is a hitman for the mafia boss" I said. "What did you do with the gun?" she asked. "I put it in my desk" I said. "Bring it home with us, we might need it" she said. "That's just great, another hitman is on our ass" I said. "When will this ever stop?" Natally asked. "I am sick of having to look over my shoulder every time I go out" she continued.

Chapter 10
Escaped

"Hey, watch where you're going, where do you think you are? A country club?" an inmate said as the mafia boss bumped into him. "What did you say to me? Do you know who I am?" he asked. "No and I don't care" the inmate said. The inmate walked to his cell and found another inmate waiting for him in his cell. The inmate pulled out a knife and stabbed him in the chest. "Never disrespect the mafia boss, you hear?" he asked as he pushed the inmate onto his bed.

He wiped the blood off his knife with the inmate's shirt and walked out of his cell and into his own. "Alright, lights out" one of the prison guards shouted. The guard walked up to the mafia boss's cell. "Lights out George" he said as he banged his nightstick on the bars. The prison guards walked down the stairs and left the building. One of them shut the lights off, making the whole prison dark.

"Morning you maggots" Harold, the lead prison guard yelled as they all walked down the aisles banging on the cell bars the next morning. Harold pushed a button that opened all the cell doors. "Okay, let's go, move it" he yelled as all the prisoners walked down the stairs and into the dining room. Another inmate, Peter, walked up to George and sat down at his table.

"Did you hear what happened to Harry last night?" he asked. "The kid got stabbed, Harold found him dead in his bed this morning" he continued. George turned to Peter. "Get out of here" he said as Peter got up and left. Frank sat down next to George. "Morning boss" he said. "What did I tell you?" he asked. "I told you to make sure you kill him in the dining room so the guards will think it was a group fight" he said. "Sorry boss" Frank said.

"I wasn't thinking" he said. "Damn right you weren't thinking" George said as he pounded on the table. "I can't put up with this kind of stupidity" he said as he got up and walked outside into the courtyard. Frank ran after him. "Let me make it up to you" he said. "What do you need?" he asked. "I need to get out of this prison" George answered.

"I need you to be my eyes and ears" George said. "I need you to tell me the prison guards' rotation schedule" he continued. Frank nodded and ran away. George started walking around, seeing if he could find any way out. Harold walked up to him. "What are you doing?" he asked. "I'm just walking around, minding my own business" George replied.

"No you're not, you're looking for an escape route. Well keep looking, because you won't find one" Harold said as he walked away. "Alright ladies, inspection time" Harold said as he signaled to the other guards. They went into every cell and tore them apart looking for anything that could be used as a weapon. One guard was tearing apart Frank's cell and found a note pad with all the guards names and times on it.

"What is this maggot?" he asked. "Nothing" Frank said. "Doesn't look like nothing" he continued. He motioned for the other guard to come over. They took out their nightsticks and started beating him. He collapsed to the ground as they continued to hit him. "That's enough" Harold said. They lifted him up, he was limp, they beat him too hard. "You idiots" Harold yelled.

"Now you're going to have to take him out back and dig a grave" he continued. They drug him across the floor and down the stairs, causing his head to bounce up and down. His body past by George's cell. "Oh boy, there goes plan A" he said as he put his hand on his forehead. The guards came back in and finished the cell searches, but didn't find anything.

The next day George was sitting on the floor in the corner of the courtyard as a guard came up to him. The guard poked him with his nightstick. "Hey, you should be out there with the rest of those maggots" he said. "Leave me alone, I'm thinking" George said. "Thinking? What the hell do you have to be thinking about, you will be in here for life" the guard said.

The guard raised his nightstick as George grabbed it from him and beat him to the ground with it. George got up and threw the nightstick on top of the guard's body as he walked away. A guard spotted the dead body and sounded the alarm. Harold made all the inmates line up side by side.

"Who is responsible for killing one of my guards?" he asked as he waited for an answer. "No answer huh?" he asked. "Well then, I have no choice but to punish you all" he said. "A week in your cells" he said as all the prisoners turned to each other and started yelling. The guards escorted the prisoners to their cells. Harold pushed a button that closed all the doors.

Harold opened up the cell doors a week later and all the prisoners stepped out. "Who killed my guard?" he asked. Silence filled the air for a number of minutes. "Make it two weeks this time" Harold said as another guard closed the cell doors. "Why don't you just tell Harold the truth" one of the prisoners yelled. Harold opened the cell doors two weeks later.

"So, who killed my guard?" he asked. "Your momma" one of the prisoners said. "Fine, you want to be funny, how about a month in your cells, that's pretty funny huh?" he asked as he closed the cell doors.

All they could do was wait until the month was up. When the month was up, some of the prisoners weren't the same. "So, I hope you learned your lesson, who killed my guard?" Harold asked.

A few moments later George stepped forward. "Did you kill my guard?" he asked. "Yes sir, I did" he said as Harold hit him in both legs with his nightstick. George dropped to his knees. "Get him out of here" Harold said to his other guards. They drug him off to an empty room and took out their nightsticks.

"I'm going to enjoy this" one of the guards said as he smacked his nightstick against his hand. The other two guards walked up behind him. They rushed George from the side. George kicked one in the stomach, sending him flying back five feet into a metal pole that was sticking out of the wall. He spat up blood as his body went limp.

George wacked the other guard in the face with an elbow strike, followed by a left punch to the throat. The guard crumbled to the floor, George took the guard's nightstick and smashed him in the face. The third guard took out his gun. "Let's see you fight your way out of this" he said. George heard a shot and looked down. He was okay and then he looked at the guard. The guard had a hole in his forehead and he dropped to the ground with a thud.

George looked up towards the door and saw Curtis shaking with a gun in his hand. "Thank you" he said as he gave him a pat on the back. "Quick, we have to do something before the other guards come" he said as they both ran to open the other prisoners' cells. As they pressed the button to open the cells, the guards came running at them with their nightsticks in the air.

The fight lasted for three days. The guards were outnumbered, but managed to kill a lot of the prisoners. At the end of three days, all the guards were dead. The prisoners that lived celebrated. One of them shot his gun at the roof, thinking that it would go through, but the bullets bounced back and killed him. "Where are you going to go?" Curtis asked George. "That is none of your business" he said.

"I thought that we could team up" Curtis said. "Listen, thank you for saving my life, but if you follow me, I will kill you" George said as he looked for a way out. He found a door, opened it and it led to a huge staircase. He started to climb it. He climbed for fifteen minutes before he reached a hatch at the top. He turned it, but it wouldn't open.

It must be locked from the outside, he thought. He took a grenade out of his pocket that he found on one of the guards and attached it to the hatch. He pulled the pin, slid down the ladder and ran as fast as he could. The grenade blew the hatch right off. He waited until the smoke cleared and climbed up again. He reached the top and stuck his head out, he was on the top of a mountain

He started to climb down the side of the mountain. He started to slip and he slid towards the edge of a cliff. He started to pick up speed and then he crashed into a rock that was protruding out. "That was close" he said as he rubbed his arm. He looked over the edge and saw that more guards were climbing up the mountain. George waited until they were close to him and kicked them off the mountain. "Ahhhhhhh" they screamed as they fell. Once George reached the bottom, he had to figure out where he was.

He walked a bit and then he started to notice familiar things around him. "I must get on a plane and go to Sweden to take care of Natally and Ryan" he said. He hitched a ride to the airport and went up to one of the tellers. "When is your next plane to Sweden?" he asked. "Not until later tonight sir" the lady behind the counter said. "Great, I'll buy a ticket" he said as he handed her some money. "While you wait, you are welcome to stay in one of our lounges" she said.

He went into the lounge and sat down at the bar. "What can I get for you sir?" the bartender asked. "I'll have a rum and coke" he said. The bartender placed it in front of him and walked away. He looked up at the television and the news was on. *In other news, there was a prison break in the Shing Tin Penitentiary late last night, all the guards were killed and all the prisoners, except for one that is unaccounted for.* They showed a picture of George. "Hey, that guy looks a lot like you" a guy across the bar said. "It must just be a coincidence, either that or you're drunk" George said.

As George got up to leave, the guy across the bar saw the same burn marks on him as was on the guy in the picture. "It is you" he yelled. "Police" the man screamed as George ran to the plane. "Enjoy your flight" the lady said as she ripped his ticket and closed the door to the entrance of the jet way.

Two police officers ran up to her. "Have you seen this man" they said as they held up a picture of George. "Yes, he just boarded the plane, but you can't get him, the plane is taking off" she said. "So, why are you going to Sweden?" the passenger beside George asked. "Business" he answered.

"What do you do?" he asked. "I am a consultant" he answered. "Consulting what?" he asked. "You ask a lot of questions buddy" George said. "I'm interested in knowing" he said. "If I told you, I'd have to kill you" George said as he laughed. "So…" he started to say as George wacked him in the throat with the side of his hand.

The plane landed and he got off. "Enjoy your stay in Sweden" the lady at the counter said as he walked by. "Now I just need to find out where Natally and Ryan are" he said. He walked down the street. He had an idea that they might have a Kung Fu school, because Kara's dad had one.

He walked downtown. "What is the best Kung Fu school around?" he asked some Chinese men. "*The Flying Tiger* is pretty good, but if you want a great school you should try *The Dark Panther*" one of the men said.

"Great, I'll check out both" he said as he got directions for them and left. He walked into *The Flying Tiger*. "Can I help you?" a student asked him. "Are your teachers Ryan and Natally?" he asked. "No, our teacher is David" the student said. He turned and walked out the door. He walked for a while, until he saw a building with a sign that read *The Dark Panther*.

"This is it" he said as he pulled on the door. "Damn, it's locked" he said as he rattled it. He climbed the side of the building and waited on the roof for us. Four hours later we pulled up to the back of the school. We opened the door, got out and started walking to the front of the building. I stopped dead in my tracks. "What's wrong?" Natally asked.

"I have a strange feeling that someone is watching us" I said as I looked up. "There's nobody there" she said as she looked up. "Come on, you're being paranoid" she said as she unlocked the door. "Ya, you're probably right" I said as I followed her inside and we went to our office.

"I was thinking of having class on the roof tonight. I am going to go up there and get it ready" I said as I walked out of the office and up the staircase to the roof. I walked onto the roof and started to move things around. We need a mat, I thought.

I went back downstairs, grabbed a mat and laid it out in the middle of the roof. I heard footsteps and looked around. "Natally?" I asked. "No, not Natally" George said as he walked out from behind a cement wall with a gun pointed at me.

"George, I thought you were in…" I said as he cut me off. "Jail" he said. "I got out, it seems they let you leave when you kill them" he continued. "Well, this is it Ryan, any last words?" he asked. "Ya, drop the gun and fight me like a man, or are you afraid you're going to lose?" I asked. "I'm not afraid of you" he said as he threw the gun across the roof.

"You are going to wish that I did shoot you" he said as he slowly stepped forward. He crouched down into a stance and brought his hands into a cover position. I stepped back into a right fighting stance, with my hands in a cover position. I signaled for him to come towards me with my right hand.

He rushed over to me throwing punches. I blocked them all and stepped back even further. "What's the matter? Are you running away?" he asked, trying to taunt me. I lunged at him with a right heel thrust kick to his chest. He flew back six feet and fell to the ground. He got up, ran at me and threw two upper cuts, which hit me, sending me backwards as I smacked my head on the ground.

I got up, shook my head and jumped up and down to try to shake off the pain. I started to circle walk around him. He ran up to me, threw a right punch as I did an inside change. He threw a left punch as I did an inside change. He threw punches until he got tired. When I saw that he was getting tired, I grabbed his arm, turned my body to the side and threw a side kick which hit him in the ribs, sending him crumbling to the ground.

"You had enough yet?" I asked. "Because I'm just getting started" I continued. He stood to his feet and wiped the blood from his face with his arm. The roof door opened. "Are you okay? You have been up here for a while" Natally said. "Natally look out" I yelled as George pushed her face first into a concrete slab, knocking her unconscious.

"Nooooo, Natally" I yelled as I ran up to George and swept his feet. He fell to the ground, I got on top of him and started to punch him in the face. He managed to throw me off of him and ran for his gun. As he grabbed his gun, I stepped on his hand. "Ahhhhhh" he yelled as he clung to his gun.

"You coward, you can't even fight without relying on a gun" I said as I kicked him in the stomach and he flipped over on his back. "Go ahead, finish me off" he said as he laid there. "I am not like you, I don't kill people, even if they do deserve it" I said as I ran to Natally. "Natally, Natally, wake up" I said as I stroked her hair, but she just laid there motionless.

"Looks like your little girlfriend is dead" George said as he laughed. "Shut up you bastard" I yelled as I hugged her tight. "Ryan? What happened?" she asked as she opened her eyes. "Natally, thank god" I said with a sigh of relief. "Ryan, look out" she said as George stood up and pointed his gun at me. "Stand up and turn around with your hands up" he said as I slowly turned around.

"You might not be willing to take a life, but I am" he said. A shot was fired and George dropped to the ground. I turned around and saw Natally holding a gun. "I bet you're glad I kept this gun with me" she said. "I'm very glad" I replied. I ran over to her and kissed her. "Are you okay?" I asked. "I'm fine" she said. "I'm going to take you to the hospital just in case, you hit your head pretty hard" I said. I picked her up, carried her to the car and drove to the hospital.

An hour later, a doctor came out of her room and up to me. "She's fine, she just has a bump on her head, but nothing serious. You can go in and see her if you like" he said. "She is okay to go home with you" he continued. "Thank you doctor, that's great to hear" I said as he walked away. I went in and held her hand.

"The doctor said you're going to be fine" I said. "Great, let's get out of here" she said as we walked down the hall and out the front door. "I am going to tell the students that there will be no class today" I said. "Won't they be disappointed?" Natally asked. "Yes, but after what we went through, we could use a day off" I said as we walked to the car.

I drove back to *The Dark Panther* and put a sign on the window that said, *no class today.* I got back in the car and we drove home. "Why don't you go sit outside in the backyard and I will make us some tea" I said. "Okay" she replied as she walked to the backyard. I opened the back door with two cups of tea in my hands.

"Okay I got the tea" I said as I looked up. I saw Jeff holding Natally in a head lock with a gun pointed to her head as I dropped the tea. "Put the gun down Jeff" I pleaded. "It's over, George is dead" I said. "It's not over until I finish the job" he said as he started to walk backwards. Two police men were walking in the alley and saw Jeff holding a gun to Natally's head.

"Freeze, put the gun down now and turn around with your hands up" one officer said. Jeff released Natally, turned around and shot one of the officers. The other officer shot Jeff in the head three times. Jeff's body fell to the ground with a thud. "Are you two okay?" the officer asked. "We are now, thanks to you" I said as he picked his partner's body up and carried him away.

"Holy cow, what a day" Natally said. "Are you hurt?" I asked. "No" she replied. "Now, let me remake that tea, I'll be right back" I said as I went back into the kitchen. I came back out and handed her a cup. "Thank you" she said as we sat down. "I was thinking that we should go on a vacation" I said.

"Where would we go?" she asked. "I want to go to Bora Bora" I said. "That sounds magical, but what about the school?" she asked. "We'll just close it down for a few weeks like we did before" I said. "Great, when are we going?" she asked. "Next week" I said. "I will tell our students tomorrow" I continued. "That's a great plan" she said as she got out of her chair and sat next to me.

The rest of the day we just sat outside, talked and listened to the birds. "We have to do something with Jeff's body" Natally said. "Ya, I suppose we should bury him" I said. "Wait for me in the car, I am going to grab a shovel from the house" I said. "Okay" she said as she went to the car. I came out with a shovel. "Let's roll" I said as we drove out into the country.

"This looks like a good spot" I said as we stopped beside a ditch. I drug his body out and threw it on the grass. I started to dig, when a police car drove by. He looked out his window and saw the shovel in my hand and the body on the ground. He flipped on his siren and drove down into the ditch and stopped in front of us. "Hands up" he yelled as he pointed his gun at me.

"What do you think you two are doing?" he asked. "I can explain officer" I said. "Well, I hope so for your sake" the officer said. "See what happened was, this man was in our backyard about to kill my girl. Two officers passed by and one of them shot him. He was just lying in our yard and we thought that we should bury him out here in the country" I said.

"Let me see if your story checks out" the officer said as he spoke into his radio. "Any officer had a confrontation with a man today and shot him?" he asked. There was silence over the radio for a few moments. "I did earlier, I had to take a guy down who was holding a female hostage and tried to shoot me" he said. "Roger that" the officer said. "It turns out you were telling the truth after all" he said. "You folks have a good day, make sure you bury him good" he continued as he got in his car and left.

An hour later the hole was dug, I threw him in and shoveled dirt on him. "Would you like to say anything?" I asked as I padded the dirt with my shovel. "Ya, burn in hell you bastard" Natally said. "Well said" I agreed as she walked up to the grave and spat on it. We got in the car and drove home.

"I'm going up to bed, I am tired" Natally said as she kissed me and walked upstairs. "I went back outside, sat in my chair and watched the moon as I went over ideas in my mind. I gave a sigh of relief, I was so glad that everything was over and that Natally and I were finally safe. It was so peaceful out, that I closed my eyes and fell asleep. I opened my eyes and saw Natally standing in front of me.

"Where you out here all night?" she asked. "Ya, I think so, I closed my eyes and like that, I was out like a light" I said. She handed me a cup of coffee. "Weren't you cold?" she asked. "No, it was beautiful" I said as I took a sip. "Want to spar a little?" she asked. "Sure, just let me finish my coffee" I said.

"I'm excited about going to Bora Bora, are you?" I asked. "Ya, I sure am, I started packing already" she said. I put down my cup and stood up. "Okay you ready?" I asked. "Yes, I am" she said as we started to spar. We started slow and then slowly got faster and faster. After half an hour we stopped. "What do you want to do with George's body, we can't just leave it up there" she said. "Ya, good point, let's just toss him in the street and let the police worry about it" I said.

We got in the car and drove to *The Dark Panther*. "I'll need some help carrying him out" I said. "Okay" she said as she followed me up to the roof. I picked up his head and she picked up his feet. We walked to the car and threw him in the trunk. We drove to the edge of the city, threw him on the side of the road and drove back to *The Dark Panther*.

"Should we tell the students what happened?" Natally asked. "No, it would only freak them out" I said. "Well, we have to tell then what happened to Jeff, they will be wondering where he went" she said. "We'll just tell them that he wasn't disciplined enough and left" I said. "Okay, if you say so" she replied. "They might not even ask" I said.

"If they don't ask, we don't have to tell them" I continued. The students began to walk in the doors and headed for the change rooms. "Why was *The Dark Panther* closed yesterday?" Simmer asked. "Personal obligation" I replied as they nodded. "Alright guys, get into your left fighting stance and close your eyes" Natally said as they all obeyed.

"I want you all to stay like this for a few moments" she continued. "You're going to picture an opponent in front of you, he is punching you. When I call the number one, he is going to deliver a right punch and you are going to block it with your left hand. When I call the number two, he is going to deliver a left punch and you are going to block it with your right hand.

"Now I want each of you to face each other and one is going to be the attacker and the other is going to be the defender" I said. "One" I said as the attacker punched with the right and the defender blocked with the left.

"Two" I said as the attacker punched with the left and the defender blocked with the right. "One, two, one, two, one, two" I called as they did it.

"Now I want you to switch so the attacker is now going to be the defender and the defender is going to be the attacker" I said. "One, two, one, two, one, two" I called. "Good job everyone" I said as they all faced me again. "I need a volunteer" Natally said as hands went up into the air. "Mmm, Josh, come up here" she said as he came forward. "There are two ways that you can deflect a kick. One way is to block with your hand. You can do this, but it takes time. Josh I want you to kick me" she said as he kicked.

Natally blocked the kick with her hand. "When I block with my hand, I am opening up my stomach for an attack. The other way to deflect a kick is to just lean your knee forward and jam your opponent's kick, Josh, kick me" she said as Josh kicked her and she used her knee to deflect it. "This way is less time consuming and more effective" she said. "Now I want you guys to try it. Go back to what you were doing before and one person kick and the other one block" she said.

After a few minutes, she stood in front of the class. "See, what did I tell you? When you use your knee to deflect a kick, it is better and you still have both your hands ready to react to whatever your opponent does. Everyone sit down on the ground" I said as I sat and they all followed. "We are going to close *The Dark Panther* for a few weeks, we are going to go on a vacation" I said. "What are we going to do?" Windy asked.

"I want you all to practice with each other while we're gone" Natally said. "Where are you going?" Pretty asked. "Bora Bora" Natally said. "We will be back before you know it, we just really need a vacation" she said. "So, we'll see you all in a few weeks" I said. "Okay, goodbye, have fun" the students said as they went to the change rooms. Natally and I waved to them as they walked out the door. "Now we have to tell Roy" I said.

I walked out the door as Natally followed after me. "I want to come too" she said. "Fine" I said as we opened the door to *The Black Cup*. We walked to the back, where Roy's office was and found him sitting in his chair. "Roy? Can I talk to you?" I asked. "Sure Ryan, what's up?" he asked. "I was wondering if Natally and I could get some time off for vacation?" I asked.

"Oh, I don't know, how much were you thinking?" he asked. "A few weeks" I said. "I'll have to call in some part timers, but ya you can, you two are great workers" he said. "Wow, thank you Roy, we really need this vacation" I said. "I'm glad I could help" he said as he turned and went back to work. I walked out of his office and gave Natally a thumbs up. She jumped up and down. "Yes" she yelled as we walked out the door and got into the car.

"So when are we leaving?" she asked. "Just as soon as I'm done packing, which won't take me long. Why don't you grab a cup of tea, go sit outside in the backyard and wait for me?" I asked as I went upstairs. She sat outside with her tea, sipping it slowly until she was halfway done. "Okay, ready?" I asked. "You bet I am" she said as she jumped up and brought her cup inside. A few moments later we got in the car and drove to the airport.

Chapter 11
The Legend Continues

We handed the lady our tickets and walked on the plane. "I want the window seat" I said. "Fine" Natally said as I passed by her and sat down. "There, you happy?" she asked. "Very" I replied as I put both arms on the arm rests. "In just a few hours, we'll be in Bora Bora" she said as she smiled. "Ya, pretty exciting" I said. "Please fasten your seatbelts folks, we're about to take off" the pilot said over the intercom.

As the plane began to climb, Natally grasped the arm rests hard. "You nervous?" I asked. "Ya, I never know what to expect" she said. "Relax, just breathe" I said. "It is just taking off and landing that bother me, the rest of the time I'm okay" she said. We finished climbing and started to level out.

"There, that's better" she said. "Would you two like anything to drink?" the flight attendant asked. "Yes, we'll have two green teas" I said. She reached into her cart. "Here you go" she said as she handed us two bottles. "Thank you" Natally said. "I'll be by later to check on you two" the flight attendant said as she walked to the next passenger.

I turned over to Natally. "Do you want something to read?" I asked. "No thanks, I'm going to take a nap" she replied. I opened my book and started reading. I looked over at Natally a while later and saw that she was in a deep sleep. I rang the bell to signal the flight attendant.

"Could I get a pillow for her?" I asked as I pointed to Natally. "Sure you can, I'll be right back" the flight attendant said as she walked to the back. She walked up to me a minute later. "Here you are" she said. "Thank you" I replied as I gently picked up Natally's head and slid the pillow underneath. I got up and went to the bathroom. A while later I came out of the bathroom and started to walk back to my seat. I saw a guy sitting in my seat.

I got insanely angry, my first thought was that he was another hitman. I walked up to him. "What are you doing" I asked with an intense look on my face. "Well hi there mister" he said as he slurred his words. Than it dawned on me that this guy wasn't a hitman, he was just drunk and he just couldn't remember where his seat was. "Alright pal, time for you to go" I said. "I am not going anywhere, I have a right to be here" he said.

"This is my seat, you have to move" I said as I started to raise my voice. I grabbed his arm and he pushed me with the other arm. I thought to myself, I could forcefully remove him, but I'll let the flight attendant handle it. I called the flight attendant over and three of them came. "This man is drunk and he is in my seat, I want him gone" I said as they nodded.

"Come on sir, you have to go" they said. "No, I'm not going nowhere" he said. Two of them grabbed him by each foot and one of them grabbed him by the shoulders. They carried him back to his seat and sat him down. "There you go, your nice and comfortable chair" one of the flight attendant's said.

"We are now starting to make our descent towards Bora Bora, I would like to thank all you folks for choosing to fly with us. We wish that you have a peaceful and relaxing time while you're here" the pilot said on the intercom. We landed, the flight attendant opened the plane door and we all walked out into the airport. "Wow, it's beautiful here" Natally said as she looked out the window at the swaying palm trees.

"Where are we staying?" she asked as we walked out the front door of the airport. "It's called *Luscious Stay*, it got great customer reviews" I said. "Great" Natally said as we walked to a cab and got in. "*Luscious Stay* Hotel please" I said to the driver as he started driving. I paid him and gave him a tip when we got there. "Thanks a lot" he said as we got out and looked at the hotel. "Wow, it's beautiful and it's right on the beach" Natally said as she smiled. "I thought you would like that" I said. "So, when we open the back door, we are right on the beach" I said as she threw her arms around me and kissed me.

We checked in at the front desk. "Enjoy your stay" the girl said from behind the counter. "Thank you, we will" Natally said as we waited for the elevator. We got to the suite and opened the door. "Wow, it's huge, it is bigger than they said it was" I said as we threw our suitcases on the bed.

We went back downstairs and out the lobby door. We walked down the street, everyone was wearing shorts and sandals. "Wow, the air is so fresh, I really feel like I can breathe here" Natally said as she took deep breaths. Everyone was so friendly, they all said hello when we passed by. "I would love to live in a place like this" Natally said as she turned to me and saw me nodding. On the corner of some of the streets, there were musicians, it felt like paradise. We walked on the white sand beach, while the water brushed up against our ankles.

That night we went out for dinner at a place called *Island Cuisine*. We walked in. "For two?" the girl asked from behind the podium. "Ya" I said. "Follow me please" she said as we followed behind her. "Here you are" she said. "Thank you" I said as we sat down. "Our special today is king crab with scallops" she said as she got out her notebook. "Can I grab you anything to drink?" she asked.

"Yes, I will have a green tea" I said. "And I will have a coconut water" Natally said as the girl wrote it down. "I'll be back in a moment with those drinks for you" she said as she walked away. We both picked up our menus and started to look at them. "It all looks good" I said a few moments later. The girl came back with our drinks. "There you go, have you decided what you want?" she asked. "Yes, I will have your special" I said. "And I will have your salmon and rib combo" Natally said. "Okay, great" she said as she wrote our orders down and picked up the menus.

A while later she came back and handed us our meals. "Anything else I can get for you?" she asked. "No, we're good" I said as she walked off. "Oh boy, this looks good" Natally said. "Ya and it will be good" I said as we started to eat. "Wow, I couldn't eat another bite" I said as I pushed my empty plate away from me. "How was yours?" I asked. "Amazing" Natally said. The girl came by and grabbed our plates.

"Would you guys like to see a dessert menu?" she asked. "No thanks, just the check" I said as she went to grab it. "How did you like it?" she asked as she handed me the bill. "Very good, we don't get food like that every day" Natally said. "Where you guys from?" she asked. "Sweden" I replied. "Really? Wow" she said.

"Are you guys enjoying yourselves here?" she asked. "Ya, we've only been here for a day, but already we are in love with it" I said. "That's great, enjoy your stay" she said as she handed us our receipt and walked away.

We walked out of the restaurant and walked on the beach for an hour. We got back to the hotel and went up to our suite. We made some tea and went out on the balcony to drink it. "Look at the moon" Natally said as I looked up. It was so big and shining so bright.

The next morning, we left the hotel and walked right onto the beach. We spent the whole morning lying on the sand and swimming in the water. "We should totally live here" Natally said as we were lying on the beach. "It is wonderful here" I said. "So is that a yes?" she asked. "Well, it's not a no" I said as I turned and kissed her. "Let's check out some of the hiking trails" she said as she jumped up.

"Ya, okay" I said as we went to the suite to change and looked up some hiking trails. "Oh, let's do that one" she said as she pointed to *Pretty Lake Trail* on the map. We walked down the street for a while until we entered a forest. We walked up hill for three hours. "I have to stop for a minute" Natally said as she pulled out some water. "It's a good thing we brought extra water" I said as she nodded.

"Okay ready?" I asked. "Yes" she said as she started to walk again. We walked up hill for another three hours, finally we reached the top. "It's beautiful" she said as we looked out and saw mountains surrounded by the clear blue ocean. "Ya, that's it, we're moving here" I said as I put my arm around Natally. We stayed at the top for an hour and then started walking down. "Watch your step" I yelled as Natally was about to trip on a protruding root. "That was so much fun" I said as we reached the bottom of the hill.

I couldn't believe it, two weeks flew by so fast. "I can't believe we have to go home today" Natally said. "I want to stay here" she continued. "Don't worry, we'll come back soon" I said as we started to pack. "Honey we have to go, the cab is waiting for us downstairs" I said as I opened the suite door. We walked down the hall, got in the elevator and checked out with the girl behind the counter.

"Please come back real soon" she said as she handed me our receipt. We threw our luggage into the trunk of the cab and got in. We walked into the airport and waited at our gate for our plane. The plane ride back felt so short. Before we knew it, we were back in Sweden.

We left the airport and drove home. "I want to go back" Natally said. "Ya, me too" I said as we looked for a hotel to stay at until we bought another house. A week later we bought the house of our dreams. "Why don't you take a shower and I will make us some tea" I said. "Okay" Natally said as she walked upstairs.

I sat out in the backyard waiting for her. She came out half an hour later holding her stomach. "I don't feel good at all" she said. "What do you think it is?" I asked. "I don't know, but I threw up" she said. "Tomorrow I will take you to the doctor" I said as I handed her a tea.

"Drink this, you'll feel better" I said as she took a sip and sat down. We talked for a while. "I am feeling better" she said. "I told you, the tea is good for that" I said. "It's been a long day and I'm tired, I'm going up to bed" I said as I got up. "Me too" Natally said as she followed me.

I opened my eyes the next morning and rolled over to Natally. "How are you feeling?" I asked. "Not good, I think it was the air in the plane" she said as she ran to the bathroom. "Once you're feeling like you can move, we will go to the doctor" I said. "I am going to be outside" I said as I walked downstairs. "Okay" she yelled. I sat down in my chair and listened to the birds chirping. An hour later, Natally came out back. "I'm ready" she said. "Alright" I said as I grabbed the keys and helped her into the car.

We drove to the doctor's office that was just two blocks from our house. "Can I help you?" the girl asked from behind the counter. "Yes, Natally is here to see Dr. Stine" I said. "Okay, he'll be right with you, just take a seat" she said as we both sat down in the waiting room. "Natally?" Dr. Stine asked. "Yes" she said.

"Come this way" he said as she followed him. I waited and waited for what seemed like hours. Finally Natally came out and sat down next to me. "So, what is it?" I asked. "I'm pregnant" she said with a big smile on her face. "You are? That's wonderful" I said as I hugged her.

On the way home I stopped by *The Dark Panther* and put a sign on the door that said, *class starts tomorrow evening*. I got in the car and we drove home. Throughout the day, the students came to see if *The Dark Panther* was open and saw the sign. "If you don't feel up to teaching, you don't have too" I said as I stroked her hair. "I forgot to stop in and talk to Roy and tell him that we're back" I said.

"You should go do that" Natally said as she handed me the keys. "You're not coming?" I asked. "No, I am just going to stay here and relax" she said as I turned and walked out the door. I walked in the door of *The Black Cup*. "Ryan, how are you?" Roy asked from behind the counter. "I'm good Roy" I said. "How was the vacation?" he asked. "It was incredible, we are thinking of moving there" I said.

"Really? It's that nice?" he asked. "Ya" I said. "So, you're starting back tomorrow?" he asked. "I am, but Natally isn't feeling that good, so I don't know when she is coming back" I said. "Well, whenever she starts feeling better, she can come back" he said. "Thanks Roy, have a good night" I said as I walked out the door.

"Welcome back" the students said as they came in *The Dark Panther*. "How was your trip" they all asked. "Relaxing" I replied. They came out of the change rooms and stood facing me. "Where's Natally?" Dragon asked. "She's at home, she's not feeling so well today" I said. "That sucks, tell her that we hope she gets better" he said. "Thank you, I will" I replied. "How many of you practiced while we were away?" I asked as they all raised their hands. "Great, that is what I want to hear" I said. "Okay, let's begin with a review" I said.

Six years later...

I woke up early and snuck out of bed without Natally knowing that I was gone. I went out to the backyard and meditated for half an hour and then I started to practice Kung Fu. Ashley opened her eyes and crawled out of bed. She looked out her window and saw that I was in the backyard.

She climbed down the stairs and opened the back door. She stood there watching me for a few minutes without me even knowing that she was there. "What are you doing daddy?" she asked as I stopped and looked at her. "Kung Fu sweetie" I said as her eyes shot wide open. "Wow" she said.

Made in the USA
Middletown, DE
15 August 2021